I0652950

Writer's block is **NOT** why writers fail.

How to ditch the excuses, beat the odds, and go from aspiring writer to successful author.

Karena Akhavein, PhD

Table of Contents

CHAPTER 7: EXCUSES TO ELIMINATE........ 179

CHAPTER 8: A "SYSTEM" TO ENSURE YOUR BOOK'S SUCCESS 196

CONCLUSION 203

QUIZ RESULTS 213

Introduction: True Story

"There is no greater agony than bearing an untold story inside you."
-Maya Angelou

"Write hard and clear about what hurts."
-Ernest Hemingway

"The wound is the place where the Light enters you."
-Rumi

The writer Joseph Epstein famously claimed that 81 percent of Americans feel that they have a book in them. That would be about 261 million people at any given point.

Yet statistics show that only around 172,000 people in the US claim to be employed as a writer or author. Other sources figure closer to 45, ooo. Whichever number you pick, it's still a minuscule fraction of those who say they feel a calling to write.

-Are you one of the approximately 260,828,000 people who wish they could call themselves authors, but are still stuck being aspiring writers?

-Do you feel that there is something in your way, keeping you from success?

-Maybe you've thought a lot about writing a book, but you never got started.

-Maybe you started writing, but you never finished.

-Maybe you actually finished writing a whole book, but then it never went anywhere.

 In any or all of these cases, you have probably experienced some level of pain in the form of disappointment, shame, regret, or guilt.

This book is for you.

True story...

I've wanted to be an author since I was a young teen. A few of the scenarios that have played out during my long and not always illustrious writing career are:

-I would have a great idea for a book, but I would talk myself out of it before I even started. Then I would beat myself up for not being creative.

-I would *not* prioritize my writing time, so that my writing would be rushed and not reflect the grandiose ideas in my head. And the thought that I really wasn't very talented would take hold of my heart and impact all my other work.

-I would write an entire book, and then immediately put it away, without editing it or showing it to anyone. And I would suffer with the silent knowledge that I had just wasted all of that time for nothing. I would feel resentful as hell whenever someone dared ask me how the book was going.

-I would write the book, and get mired in repeatedly self-editing, out of fear of having a "real" editor judge me. The self-loathing would then come out in all its glory, the imaginary editor in my head growing into a superhuman monster with the power to ruin my life.

-I would freeze midway through slogging through the process of writing query letters to agents, because I decided that my whole premise was lame and that my chances of getting an agent were nil. I would read other books and judge them harshly against mine, while at the same time the constant comparison would give rise to serious anxiety.

One day, miraculously, I thought, I got an agent. I paid for and went through the whole editing process. Yay, me! Actually, not yay. What did I do after that? After all that work, I essentially self-sabotaged or failed to advocate for myself to the point where my book did not get published. Something kept stopping me. I was worried by what friends and family would think of my writing. Was it intellectual enough? Was my whole idea stupid? You may have noticed the letters P, H, and D after my name on the cover of this book, but believe me, earning a Ph.D. in literature from an Ivy League institution did not help me to feel any less unqualified. You've no doubt heard of imposter syndrome. Well, I definitely had it.

The few people who had read my books encouraged me to self-publish, if I was unwilling to keep trying for a conventional publishing deal.

I liked this idea, because the idea of self-publishing is intrinsically equal opportunity. I thought it was great that authors no longer had to subject themselves to the gatekeepers present in conventional publishing.

However, the online world has its own gatekeepers. Self-published authors are subjected to mysterious and not-so-mysterious algorithms and sometimes judgmental reviews by trolls hiding behind their anonymity. The online universe is so vast, and the need for marketing and advertising oneself is more crucial than ever.

When you're a fledgling writer whose confidence has been almost completely destroyed by the process of writing, editing, and querying, you are not in the strongest position to do all of the self-promotional work that is crucial for writing success.

In my case, you may be able to guess what happened next. I ended up publishing my books under a series of pen names, and never really promoting them. They sold a paltry number of copies- only a few of my absolute closest friends even knew my books were out.

I decided that these books' lack of success was proof that I was not worthy of success.

I threw myself into other writing-related projects, but still, the dream of being an author kept resurfacing. I was too down in the dumps to launch a marketing push. But I summoned the last of my strength and parlayed it into one last, last-ditch effort at conventional publishing.

"Miraculously," I found another agent. A small but reputable publisher decided to publish my book, and so I went through the whole process of editing again. I hired an editor that sucked. Lost money and hired another editor that was fabulous. And then the publisher pulled out of the deal. And the agent ghosted me. Once again, I had crashed and burned.

Part of what happened to my book could be attributed to lazy, unprofessional, or unscrupulous agents, publishers, and editors, but honestly most of the blame for the failure of my writing career rested squarely upon my own shoulders. I didn't truly believe I could do it, so I never gave myself a fighting chance.

Throughout all of this, whether it was during my attempts at the conventional publishing process, or during my self-publishing fiasco, I kept thinking to myself that there was something wrong with me. That's why the system wouldn't work for me.

But that line of thinking really hurt, so I moved on to blaming the system. It was broken. That was why it wasn't working for me. The whole entire publishing system was completely messed up.

This line of thinking hurt too, though. Also, it didn't explain why some writers were still making it.

The worst part: feeling powerless to succeed in the one thing that mattered most to me.

Finally, after doing a lot of soul-searching- after taking a cold hard look at my own psyche and my own ego, I started to see the reality of the situation. I started to identify the things that were truly holding me back. Sure, the publishing industry is fundamentally flawed, but my much more important discovery was that there were mental blocks that hobbled me from the very beginning of the writing process to the very end. These blocks were causing me real pain.

I decided that the only way of actually feeling better was by fixing what was causing me pain, small point by small point, and moving forward.

After a lot of trial and error, I started to figure out the specific things that would work for me. I assembled these things into a system. I decided that the method I was starting to devise would probably work on other writers, as well, so I started meeting with and communicating with thousands of writers just like me.

When I say, "just like me," I mean that I found a very disturbing common point. No matter where we were in our journeys, many of us did not feel successful enough to call ourselves authors. Some of us still described ourselves as "aspiring writers." Sometimes, we managed to refer to ourselves as "writers" or "working writers," but "successful author"? That is a descriptor we reserved for the blockbusters, the household names, best-selling authors such as Stephen King, Dan Brown, and JK Rowling. Some insisted that they were authors or "working authors" or "working writers," but I could detect a defensive edge, a little peek at the ego that made these writers feel, deep down, that they weren't quite as successful as they insisted they were. According to them, they didn't need support or advice.

Then why were they hanging out at these events or in these chat rooms, or on these message boards?

One day, I happened to find myself in conversation with a group of fellow "aspiring writers," and one of them- and I wish I could remember her name because she truly changed the course of my life- opened my eyes.

"We're so ridiculous," she said. "In other people's opinions, so many of us are already successful. Many of us have done *almost* everything we needed to do to be successful as we define it. What's blocking us? It's not the normal definition of writer's block. Why don't we actually complete that tiny last part of the process? There must be something wrong with our mindset!"

That's when the lightbulb went off. I had thought that the fact that inspiration was rarely a problem when I was writing meant that I didn't have writer's block.

But I *did* have writer's block. I had writer's block, because there was obviously a very real obstacle to my writing success. This was a great thing to realize. However, none of the many books or articles I had consulted addressed my specific blocks. They didn't delve into the *real* writer's block.

What is the REAL writer's block?

The *real* writer's block is one or more internal barriers that prevent you from achieving writing success, pure and simple. It can stop you in your tracks at *any* stage in your writer's journey.

I began to analyze my problem further. Yes, there was something wrong with my mindset, and this was preventing me from doing the things that would directly impact my success. This, in turn, was causing me pain. Intense pain. The shameful pain of failure, the embarrassing pain of not finishing what I had sworn to all my friends and family I would actually finish, the sad, regretful pain of seeing my dream retreat even further.

Eventually, I figured out how exactly my mindset was causing my writer's block. Once I admitted the specific pain that it was causing me, I was able to finally use that information and that uncomfortable sensation to build the motivation I needed to spring back into action, to keep moving forward.

Releasing my specific writer's blocks led me to not only finish and better promote my fiction work, but also to see bigger, and to modify my initial strategy and vision. I founded Spalmorum, along with my writing group, my YouTube channel, and coaching business, as a direct result of this work on myself, and because of the discrepancy I found between how many people *wish* they could write a book, and how many actually *do*, of how many people "have a book in them" but never let it get out. Of how many people dream of being an author but never complete the simple series of actions needed to truly see their wishes come true.

I founded Spalmorum on the sincere belief that every single one of us is *capable* of becoming a successful author, given the right impetus. Oddly enough, it is writer's block that will provide that impetus.

How?

That thing standing between you and writing success is the real writer's block. We're not talking about the conventional, too-narrow definition of writer's block. No. Writer's block is not merely a temporary loss of inspiration. It is not just not knowing what to write about, or not being able to finish your book. It is much more serious than that. It is deep-seated, and it is *painful.*

That *pain* is part of the solution.

As human beings, pain is a signal that tells us that something is unequivocally *wrong.*

The principal quality of pain is that it demands attention.

Pain demands an explanation. It's uncomfortable. You can't just ignore it. It forces you to do something about it. Pain is a motivator. It's what usually convinces us to act, to *do* something: to go to the doctor, to stop doing something that's bad for us.

"Managing" pain or "medicating" is never the ideal long-term solution. With some physical ailments, eradicating pain completely is not a possibility. However, in the case of pain caused by writer's block, you can 100% address it and fix what's wrong.

This book will as a matter of course address the writer's block that so many other books and articles discuss. This is the writer's block that manifests itself early in the process: the lack of inspiration, the faulty time management, the feeling of being stuck when trying to flesh out a scene.

However, unlike most other books on writer's block, we are also going to examine the deeper issues that prevent you from being a successful author in the long run. We're going to dive deep into the self-defeating mindsets that affect you in all stages of the writing process. We're going to address what to do if you've always had the desire to write, but it never actually translated into an actual manuscript. We're going to help you to overcome the self-doubt and loss of momentum that arrives in the "mushy middle" of your book. We're going to help you to keep moving forward with the important phase that comes *after* you've finished your first draft.

The Spalmorum Method is my solution for writer's block. It is a direct result of my trial and error. It is a holistic approach to curing writer's block. It finds and eliminates the *specific* obstacles that trip up a writer on the path to success, and gives you targeted support, information, inspiration, and motivation. It permanently transforms your mindset, to overhaul your approach to writing for good.

The Spalmorum Method

Forces radical self-honesty.

Identifies your specific blocks and makes you aware of the resulting pain.

Eliminates or reframes problem mindsets to remove blocks and force action, relieving the pain and moving you towards success.

Breaks down any residual excuses.

Prevents writer's blocks from resurfacing.

Is it that simple? Yes, but it is not simplistic. I need to take you through it in more detail.

This is not one of those books where the author claims that they used "this simple system" to sell millions of dollars' worth of books or of whatever else they're peddling. I have not sold a bestselling novel (yet). However, this approach has and will continue to take me closer and closer to my goals. This is the approach that finally allowed me to say: "Yes, I am a successful author." It's the approach that yielded this very book. It's the approach that led me to launch the Spalmorum platform, which includes a new kind of publishing company. (Yes, you can absolutely pitch me when your book is ready.)

Through Spalmorum and the Spalmorum Method, I hope to guide each author to save them time and frustration. My ultimate goal is to help create a world where more writers are empowered to tell their stories, and to put them into a format that can be enjoyed by as many people as possible, to make more readers dream, think, and feel. I will help you to get your story written, edited, formatted, published, and sold, so that you can be the author you've been wanting to be, even if you've never written fiction before, even if you have a full-time life and career.

Why the Spalmorum Method?

Why use this method rather than just sticking to the advice laid out in so many other books and articles on "beating writer's block"?

The Spalmorum Method is different. Other books, articles, and courses on the subject of writer's block always focus on "solutions." These include suggestions such as:

-Just sit down and write!

-Go outside!

-Use a timer and do writing sprints!

-Try these writing prompts!

Each of those techniques has its place and can work to some degree, and we'll be discussing them later in the book, but they usually function in a purely temporary manner, because the simple fact is, not a single one of these "fixes" addresses the *root* of the problem.

These methods work to simply "manage" or "control" or distract from the pain. They're the equivalent of taking Ibuprofen when you know damn well you should actually go to the doctor.

This book works on more fundamental issues. It addresses the real *source* of the pain and goes deeper to actually fix the issues permanently. Brand new writers will have an infinitely better chance of making the transition from aspiring writer to successful author, and in much less time, and working authors will waste less time on productivity and morale-sapping thought patterns, in order to achieve more than ever before.

Unlike books that aim to help you with the writer's block that affects you specifically during the inspiration and initial writing process, this book shows you how to implement the Spalmorum Method to help you in all of the stages of the writing process, including the most challenging ones, the ones that bookend the actual writing part that most people focus on: pre-writing and marketing.

What is *Spalmorum?*

Now that I've mentioned this very odd term a few times, I should probably go into what *Spalmorum* means.

You've probably never heard that word, right? It harks back to the early days of publishing.

Back in 1457, when "modern" printing had just been invented, and Gutenberg and his workshop were operating the first printing press in Europe, most of the printed materials were religious or political texts. Only a small percentage of the population was literate, but whenever something was printed, it would essentially go viral, being snapped up by anyone who could read. *Spalmorum* was the first printed error in a manuscript. It was meant to read "Psalmorum," meaning a compendium of Psalms, but the error was not caught by Gutenberg's team of early editors, and it made its way into a printed religious manuscript. However, despite the fact that there were only a few books in circulation at the time, meaning that *literally* every reader in town would have seen it, this mistake did not cause the publishing industry to crumble. There were no real ramifications other than, we're guessing, improved editing processes. In fact, the whole episode has all but disappeared from the annals of history.

Why did I choose to name my writing platform and my publishing house after a *mistake*?

Because making a mistake or two does not mean failing at the whole enterprise. No matter how many mistakes you've made with your writing, no matter how many false starts you've had, and dead ends you've encountered, you still have a chance to produce something that will be read by thousands of people and influence their lives. I liked the idea of naming a company after something that was reminiscent of the time of Gutenberg, because I feel that this is a similarly heady time, where new technologies and platforms are giving writers more possibilities to be heard than ever before.

Why is it so important to go through this process to try to cure all your writer's blocks, instead of giving up and doing something else, something that's less scary? Because your ideas count. Your words count. Being able to write clearly can sell your ideas, move your readers, and increase your general success. If you even thought of picking up this book, or have ever Googled "overcoming writer's block," you know that writer's block is keeping you from your purpose and robbing you and your readers from something valuable. Never succeeding is vastly more frightening, in the long run, than trying and failing.

Because failure hurts.

To me, writing is everything. Storytelling is one of the most important skills you can master. Being an author is not just about you. It's about being part of something bigger.

If you want your ideas or words to inspire others in the most direct, accurate manner, writing and then getting it in front of readers is still the way to do it. We now have a much broader choice of media for sharing our messages, but books, and especially e-books, are eminently portable, economical, and shareable. Books can delve into a subject or a story with a depth that a short story or article cannot attain. Writing a book immediately establishes you as an *authority*. As an authority, your mission is to share ideas with the world. Anything that prevents you from doing that is a negative force that will cause you pain.

The world is changing so fast, but storytelling is still what binds us together, what helps us to share our experiences, what helps us to understand each other in this crazy, noisy world. Writing helps us to make sense out of the chaos. Writing and storytelling are crucial to every venture, to every interaction, to every product launch or business. People are consuming content like never before, and there is such a variety of content that there truly is something for everyone.

First, before we even start down this road, a little reality check:

This book will not work for everyone. It will only work if you're willing to be radically honest with yourself and to actually do the work.

Will this book work for you?

-If you really, truly think you can't do it, and suspect you will never be able to shift that mindset... this book might not be able to get through to you.

-If you think this book is going to "fix" you without your needing to put in time or effort, you won't get very far. There are more efficient ways of doing things, more productive ways, and ways that will prevent you from wasting time, and this book will teach you that. But there are no shortcuts.

-If you just want to write to make a quick buck and need to monetize quickly, and think this is your tool for doing that, I'm telling you right now that, while this book may get you closer to that goal than you are now, there are probably business books out there that align better with your purpose.

-If you were never sure you wanted to be a writer, but you're kind of doing it because people (your mom and that one teacher in tenth grade) have told you that you are naturally good at writing, you're going to have to find more motivation than that before this book starts to work for you.

For this book to work:

-You will need to constantly step out of your comfort zone.

-You will need to realize that writing takes time. It takes research, practice, long hours, false starts, and do-overs.

-You will need to accept that writing success is not black and white, one size fits all, or always financial.

-You will need to give up laziness and excuses and see them for what they are.

-You will need to make the choice to write. Deciding to do anything and to follow through is always about making a choice. Making a choice means turning your back on other things. You need to do this with a clear purpose.

Why is being an author instead of forever being an aspiring writer inportant?

-Writing is a way to take your power back.

-Writing a book positions you as an expert.

-As a writer, you get to tell stories all the time without anyone calling you a liar.

-Writing helps you to make meaning out of the world.

-As a writer, you experience everything more deeply.

-Writing means pursuing a dream rather than an obligation.

-Writing is creating magic. It is making things come to life.

-As a writer, you can work anywhere and anytime.

-If you pour your heart into being a writer, you will never wonder "what if?"

Have you decided that yes, this book is going to work for you?

Yay! Let's get started. Your readers are counting on you!

-Karena Akhavein, PhD

CHAPTER 1: All about writer's block.

What is writer's block?

-Writer's block is a pain in the ass.

Ask any writer- amateur or experienced author- about the hardest part of the writing process. An overwhelming majority will answer with some glib quote about writing being somewhere between torture and fun. Sounds a little simplistic but it's true. Writing is definitely fun. But at the same time, everything about writing is hard. It is truly painful. The discrepancy between the great stuff that's in your head and your heart and the stilted, stunted version that shows up on the page is the source of major pain and frustration. Some writers work through this pain, others give up.

The important thing to realize is that, without exception, all writers experience some form of writer's block, somewhere in the process, if not at every stage in the writing process. You are not alone. Having writer's block is not a sign that you are somehow lacking or less than. It is not the symptom of some weakness that signifies that you are not meant to be an author.

Writer's block is a common pain point that can cause frustration, depression, anxiety, and anger. Writers suffering from writer's block feel worthless and powerless. They feel that they are not managing to do the main thing that they know they were put on this earth to do. Writer's block prevents writers from sharing their story with the world. There is nothing more painful than that.

-Writer's block is all in your head.

I'm not saying that writer's block is not real. It's simply that objectively, this very real, observed, and measurable phenomenon that all writers suffer from at some point or another does not stem from any outside forces. It is 100% self-created. You don't get writer's block because the weather was bad, or because someone snagged your taxi, or because someone said something mean to you- at least not directly. You get writer's block because of deeply ingrained habitual thought processes that you yourself have adopted, developed and implemented. Why in the world would you do that to yourself?

Exactly! Why would you do this to yourself? If you become conscious of this self-defeating process, if you come to understand why you are doing it and are able to identify exactly how you are doing it, you'll already be well on your way to eradicating it.

I propose that we all agree that we must get our heads out of our asses and back into the game of writing and building our writing careers, so that we can tell our stories, produce work we'll be proud of, and attain our goal of touching our readers. This will lead directly to our finding success as authors and creative entrepreneurs.

Wait, what does being a creative entrepreneur have to do with writer's block? This point is super important: I mentioned that writer's block is anything that prevents you from finishing, publishing, and promoting your book. One of the major writer's blocks affects the process of marketing your book. We'll talk quite a lot about this later.

Writer's block makes you think and do crazy things

How many of these behaviors sound familiar?

-Lurking on writing community boards on Facebook, subtly or overtly trolling other authors, or silently judging them?

-Getting frustrated because others are doing that thing we dreamed of doing?

-Seeing other authors as "competition" and growing jealous of their successes?

-Reading a book and compulsively thinking, "I could have done it better," or "why them and not me?"

-Writing something and not releasing it because we anticipate a negative reaction?

-Compulsively self-editing out of a search for that ever-elusive perfection?

-Spending more time thinking about how to deal with critics than actually writing?

-Looking at the facts and figures about the publishing industry and using them to justify your belief that it is almost impossible to encounter success as a writer.

I've done all of those things at some point, but that's not the person I wanted to be, nor the writer I wanted to be. That's not how I wanted to live my life. It was not a comfortable place to be. Being in that situation was a pain in the ass. It probably made me act like a pain in the ass, too. And it was 100% in my power to stop those self-defeating thoughts and behaviors, so I did.

Here are some of the sane, positive beliefs that I needed to adopt in order to start releasing all the blocks preventing me from writing success:

- I am a writer, and writing is important to me. Because of this, I have made, and will keep making, the decision to write, to move my writing career ever-forward.

-There are an infinite number of ideas out there, and an infinite number of ways to express them. Other writers are not the competition. They are my colleagues. We are on the same team. There is not a finite amount of success to be had. We can all be successful.

-I am a work in progress. My work is also a work in progress. Nothing is fixed, errors are fixable, and anyone or anything can improve, including me.

Once I adopted each of these ways of thinking, my writer's blocks began to disappear. The pain started to disappear. But getting to that place was not an easy road. This book is going to outline some concrete strategies for getting there much more easily than I did at the time.

Other important things to know about writer's block:

Writer's block can be experienced differently by different people

Writer's Block is your ego rearing its ugly head

Writer's block affects all writers, not just fiction writers

Anyone *can* cure their writer's block, but not everybody *will*

Writer's block will make you come up with so many excuses

You need to be vigilant to prevent writer's block from sneaking back up on you

Maybe it's not actually writer's block

We will be addressing all of these points in this book, but first, let's go over what writer's block is NOT.

What is writer's block NOT?

Writer's block is not something that only strikes during the writing part.

Being a successful author is not just about inspiration. A successful author is a creative entrepreneur who understands that a book is a product needs to be researched, sold, and marketed if it is to be successful. Many authors actually encounter a serious block not so much during the actual writing, but in other, equally crucial, parts of the process. This too is writer's block, and most other books and articles about writer's block don't address it.

I'm pretty damn sure I've experienced every type of writer's block there is. As someone who has been writing since I was a child, I figured out relatively early on, and through experience and trial and error, how to chase inspiration, how to avoid research-itis, how to motivate to write through the self-doubt. I mastered the skill of writing a whole book despite frequent episodes of crippling writer's block that left me paralyzed at my keyboard. A little secret: knowing that those episodes aren't permanent takes away a lot of their power. Besides, that type of writer's block wasn't my main issue.

Writer's block is not a "one size fits all" ailment.

All writers do not experience writer's block in the same way. This is one of the dangers of using the traditional definition of writer's block as inspiration block, or inability to get the words on the page. That type of block is rarely the actual block that prevents success. That is a fleeting state. The other blockages are much more pervasive and harder to shake. And we're all different. There are things that you will find easy as a writer, and those will be the same things that another writer finds super challenging. We each come with a different past, different experiences, different training and education, and hence we each have very unique things that will trip us up. The good news is that I've seen enough writers struggle with different parts of the writing, publishing, and promotion process that I believe I have pretty much seen all kinds of blocks. We have managed to group them into broad categories that will do a more than adequate job of addressing all but the most bizarre cases…and even if you are a truly "weird" writer whose block is absolutely unique, if you read this book with an open heart and mind, you will find something that speaks to you in it.

Writer's block is not permanent

Writer's block can go away on its own. You will be more inspired one day, less the next. Motivated one day, less so the next. And you will feel confident one day, less so the next. No matter how long you procrastinate, you will have moments when your so-called writer's block has less of a hold on you. But these natural fluctuations, while a good sign that writer's block is not necessarily here to stay, are not as good a sign as you think. As long as you let writer's block control you, you cannot beat it. Everyone has the power to stop writer's block. But not everyone will. In this book I hope to have you finding the power and the motivation to banish it for good.

Now, let's figure out which specific writer's blocks are impacting you most.

QUIZ: What Type of Writer's Block do I Have?

Take your quiz here, and get your results at the back of the book, or even better, go online or <u>click here</u> for an easier to score version of the quiz and access to a helpful worksheet.

*You can choose one, all, or some of the statements below if they have ever felt true or familiar.

1)Which statement sounds most like you?

A. I have a ton of great ideas, which makes it hard to commit to any one of them.
B. I have good ideas, and I do try to act on them, but then I don't always follow through. I eventually get stuck on the details.
C. Whenever I get an idea, it seems that either someone else has done it better than me already, or that maybe there is something better I should be doing.

2)How confident are you about your writing project?

A. I think my ideas are great, but I worry about what others will think of me when they see my final project, especially if I fail.

B. I have something great in my mind, but I fear I don't have the education/training/experience to truly succeed.

C. I dream of achieving something, but I never really follow through with it because I know the chances of success are so slim.

3)How would you describe your work and writing style?

A. Very creative. I'm an ideas person, and I'm good at the big picture. People say I'm great at brainstorming. I'm a good group leader.

B. Direct and pretty straightforward. I want to get stuff done right. Sometimes it's too short.

C. Passionate and intellectual. I do a deep dive into the process and the details. I love getting lost in my work and the words. The more complicated the better.

4)How do you feel about writing groups?

A. Sometimes love the idea, sometimes hate it. I love to share my work and brainstorm, but I also don't like others to judge my work or potentially steal my ideas. I can't help but notice that some people are better than me and some are worse.

B. I might like to work in a group more but only if it's low pressure commitment wise, and if I learn something from it. Otherwise I would rather work alone.

C. I love them! I crave the support, inspiration, and motivation, and I don't want to have to do everything alone. This forces me to do something.

5)What is your creative/writing process?

A. I get an idea and then brainstorm about it until I feel ready to start, to make a basic plan, and then I'll let it grow organically.

B. I need to create a detailed outline before I start.

C. I jump in before I'm totally ready but trust that things eventually will come together. I see where the characters will lead me.

6) When do you work on your writing?

A. Full-time, or as close to that as possible. At the very least I can say that it occupies a lot of my time and energy.

B. I can't do it full time, but I try to do a little bit every day, or on weekends. I sometimes feel like I have to play catch up a lot.

C. When inspiration strikes. If I'm not inspired, I don't work as well. I get a lot done in a short time.

7) What is your attitude towards your writing?

A. It's my passion or at least my current obsession. It's a crucial part of me. I'm either keeping it secret or telling everyone who will listen.

B. I'm treating it like a job. Right now, I'm growing my skills.

C. It's something that I would love to devote more time to. If it works out I will.

8) Where in the writing, art, or entrepreneurial process do you usually get stuck?

A. I have a hard time convincing myself to start or figuring out how to start. Once I am further in, momentum takes hold.

B. I'm fine until I hit the middle of the process, where technical things start to matter. and then everything falls apart.

C. Once the first flush of excitement is done, I have a hard time really pushing through to completion.

9)What is the hardest part about being a writer?

A. Coming up with good ideas and judgement of others.

B. All of the moving parts and the pieces and elements that go into it.

C. The time commitment and follow-through and promotion.

10)How does writer's block make you feel?

A. Alone. No one understands what I'm going through, and if I tell them they'll know I'm doing something wrong.

B. It's part of the process. It's not fun, but I know I'll get through it eventually.

C. Helpless and frustrated. How will I ever succeed if this always happens to me?

11)What is your hope for your writing?

A. I just want to get this out there, so I can have that sense of achievement and/or to show everyone who doubted me that I could do it.

B. I want to turn my passion, knowledge, and talent into a career.

C. I want to make money and/or become well known.

12) Have you finished, almost finished, or published a book before? What was your experience?

A.   I succeeded and I either want to bring that success to the next one, or have a niggling feeling that I will never achieve that level of success again.

B.   I completed or almost completed it, but it did not go as well as it could have for several reasons. Now I am a little burned out.

C.   I've tried, but failed, or I never got to the point of actually completing a full launch.

13) How do you feel about hiring outside help such as an editor?

A.   Anyone I would hire may mess up the integrity of what I'm doing. How do I know they're qualified? How do I know they won't steal some part of my concept or part of the spotlight?

B.   I can do it all myself, and/or am willing to do it myself, for free. Why waste the money?

C.   Hiring someone makes me feel that someone has my back. They'll help me to improve my work, and I don't have to do it alone.

14) What is your marketing plan for your writing?

A. If I do a good job, the customers or clients or buyers will come. I don't need to do too much.

B. I've got a strategy for that. I'm pretty good with computers, so I hope to get my platform up and running myself: website, social media, the works.

C. I've got some idea of what I need. I plan on having input but would rather someone else do a lot of it for me.

15) Do you share thoughts, fears, and ideas with others in the book industry, and other writers?

A. No way! They might steal my ideas, and I don't like to be judged!

B. Sometimes. But I worry that they think I want something from them, or that they'll think I'm out of my depth.

C. All the time! It's encouraging and inspiring!

Tally your A's, B's, and C's and check the back of the book for your block type(s)

***

You'll notice that your test results have yielded one or two or even three of the 3 types of block below:

-Lack of INSPIRATION

-Lack of INFORMATION

-Lack of MOTIVATION

Some of you may wish to skip ahead to the section or sections that concern you most, however, I recommend reading through each chapter, as we all suffer from some elements from each of these categories of block, and also, they are less straightforward than they seem. Sometimes something that looks like one kind of block actually has a different source.

In fact, there is a fourth block.

-EGO Block

Why does it not come out as one of the quiz results? Because I can guarantee with utmost confidence that you have some degree of Ego Block. I have it, and every human out there has it. The sooner you realize this and deal with it, the better. The ego is powerful. It's impossible to silence it completely, but it is possible to force it to take a time out and to play the quiet game, so you can get back to the business of writing.

Now it's time to discuss each of the blocks in further detail.

CHAPTER 2- The 3 types of writer's block

Writer's block type 1: Lack of INSPIRATION

Let's start with inspiration. Inspiration is always the first step in any creative endeavor. Makes sense, right? In order to start any creative project, or any entrepreneurial project, you must be inspired. You must feel that spark, which excites you enough to prompt you to think of embarking on a project and make the significant work it will entail worth it. Many creatives alternate between a state where they almost too full of ideas, and then times when they fear they have lost their intention.

Lack of inspiration can happen at any stage in the creative game.

When I first started my writing group, my writers were super enthusiastic. They had tons of great ideas that they couldn't wait to put into book form. Our first meeting mostly consisted of them sharing these ideas with each other and excitedly supporting each other and adding to each other's concepts. Then, their enthusiasm started flagging. Some of them had a scene or two tied to their idea, and we worked on getting those on paper. But then, I assigned homework: to flesh out the rest of the plot. The whole thing petered out at that point. My writers were suddenly completely deflated. I could feel a shift in the energy the next time our group got together. Very few of them had completed the homework. Instead, they were intent on telling me about another idea or even multiple ideas they'd had that might be so much better than the original.

This happens to so many of us. We start out with a multitude of ideas that we think are wonderful, but then, right when we begin to truly commit to one, our heads, or our egos, will convince us that our ideas are actually pathetic, that they've been done to death before, and that others have done them better. The prospect of needing to actually commit to one single idea makes our inspiration fly out the window.

Or...maybe you've found an idea you really, really like, and you're trucking along with your book, and then inspiration dries up. Suddenly, your characters seem flat. You can't figure out what happens next. The stuff you're writing doesn't do your fabulous idea justice. Basically, you stop to even see the point of what you're writing. This is also an inspiration problem, but one that appears at a different stage in the process.

This happened to me a lot throughout my writing career. I would write multiple scenes, develop my characters, even get a respectable number of words down…and then, I would get the feeling that something was off. Try as I might, I would not manage to figure out the essential last 25% of the plot or outline. This has happened to me most often in NaNoWriMo style challenges, where you force yourself to get a bunch of words down, and then those 50,000 words that you were so proud of getting down never become a finished novel.

Even finishing your book doesn't necessarily put an end to inspiration problems! Imagine this: You've gotten to the point where you've published your book, but it's not gaining traction. You've done "everything you can" to market it: Facebook, Instagram, emailing your whole list... but you didn't find as many readers as you'd hoped. Your lack of inspiration when it comes to marketing can cause you to fail to look for new and interesting avenues to promote your work. Instead, you remain focused, stubbornly so, on a single method or outlet, persuaded that there's no other way to go. Or even worse, you give up, because it's obviously not working. Also, isn't it almost impossible to sell books? (Hint: If it was impossible to sell books, other writers wouldn't be doing it every single day. You wouldn't have initially wanted to do this with a zero percent chance of success, whatever you may think now.)

The good news is, inspiration, though it may seem like a fundamental problem, is easy to address with the correct mindset.

Truth:

Almost all inspiration issues stem from the ego, from feelings of inadequacy, or fear that our genius will not be seen by others once the mediocrity of our idea is revealed.

Wrong Mindset:

I'm not excited by this idea anymore. It must mean it's bad, and not meant to be. It's not even that original. It's been done before. Better look for a better one.

Correct Mindset:

It's not so much the idea that counts, as the way you express the idea. Yes, most "ideas" have been done before. They're not that unique. But your way of expressing the idea can be unique. Your characters, your settings, your language…

Think back to how excited you were initially about this idea: that's because it speaks to you. Other people will be excited about it, too. Work on doing justice to this idea and you'll be on the right track.

Writer's block type 2: Lack of INFORMATION

Are you being held back by lack of vision and information?

The second possible source of writer's block is information, or lack thereof. There are many varieties of block brought on by lack of information, but in the most general sense, the author decides that they, for some reason, do not have the knowledge or the ability to carry out their task.

I have come across writers at all different levels of education in my career:

-The new writers who don't even know enough to know that they are missing some crucial knowledge.

-The writers who know that they are missing some of the knowledge that they might need and are a bit tentative because of it.

-The "experts" who have taken multitudes of classes and have done all of the research, and who believe that they know it all.

What do these writers have in common? Each and every one of them risks being tripped up by some aspect of information block at some point in the process.

In my writer's group, my newer writers usually ask a ton of questions. This is normal. After all, no one is born naturally knowing everything about writing and publishing a book. I want to stress that just because you have many questions does not mean that you will never know enough to write a book and make it successful. I know it's daunting, but you can learn as you go. Same goes for those of you who know something but feel that you are missing some crucial bits. Those who think they "know it all" may actually be at a bigger disadvantage because the world of publishing is always changing, and also being a successful writer isn't always all about rules.

Many authors decide to write a book without knowing anything about the publishing industry. This can be both an advantage and a disadvantage. Before you congratulate yourself for being at an advantage and forge ahead, hold on: It is a *small* advantage and a *large* disadvantage! The small advantage lies in not being frightened by the difficulties and by small odds of success, and not limiting your creativity with what you know about genre requirements and such.

Also, I've said it before: publishing is changing so quickly that many of the things that used to hold true no longer do. Writers have much more flexibility when it comes to how to publish their work or get it out there. There is conventional publishing, indie publishing houses, hybrid publishing, self-publishing, online publishing on a platform, publishing as a serial, audiobooks, or making use of platforms such as Patreon. This flexibility does not mean that anything goes. You still need to be informed as to some of the non-negotiables of writing and the things that make the difference between failure and success for an author.

Also, there are a fixed set of tasks that need to be carried out, and carried out right, for a book to do well on the market. If you start writing without knowing what these are you may think that you will be done much sooner than you actually will be and get discouraged before you are actually in a position to succeed. It has been demonstrated that, in general, humans tend to vastly underestimate the time and effort it will take them to complete a task. And when the time or effort pass a certain mark, they manage to convince themselves that they should quit. Don't let this happen to you.

Let's look at the big picture.

What does it take to write a book?

In the most general sense, it happens in 3 phases:

Beginning

This sounds obvious, but it may be the most overlooked step in the process. You write a book by deciding first why you want to write, what you're going to write, and how you're going to write it.
Then you have to decide to start writing.

Staying motivated

Once you start writing, you will face self-doubt and overwhelm and a hundred other adversaries. Planning ahead for those obstacles ensures you won't quit when they come. You need to come up with strategies that will make the task of writing a whole book easier for you.

Finishing

Nobody cares about the book that you almost wrote. We want to read the one you actually finished, which means no matter what, the thing that makes you a writer is your ability not to start a project, but to complete one. Also, if you finish a book but then never promote it, you might as well have never started.

All right, you through that was too simplistic? You have a ton of other questions? Great. Because I have heard all the questions before. Let me address them one by one.

Information block and problem mindsets parading as AUTHOR FAQ's

I love questions, and always welcome them- whether they're asked during my writing group or posed to me online. Yes, the answers to almost any question about writing can be found through a simple google search, but if there is any way I can help someone to get a faster answer from a source they trust, I am more than happy to deliver. However, in my experience, for all of the completely normal questions I get about writing and publishing, I'll get some questions that are not so innocent. Sometimes, the asker of these questions is in pain because they are having a hard time writing their book. They're blocked. They want to quit. But they need to be given permission to quit, or else it will make them hurt more. Basically, if they ask the right question, they just might get a response that will give them a really great excuse to quit. How can I tell when this is the case? When I see a writer asking the same question over and over, as if hoping to get a different answer one of the times they ask, or when a writer asks a question in a format that begs a specific response, I know that there is something else going on.

Unfortunately for the askers of these questions, I've heard enough that I won't be providing any hall passes for writing your book. However, I can tell which problem mindsets are being revealed by the line of questioning, so I can help to guide these writers to a better place. See if any of these questions sound familiar.

Question: HOW LONG DOES MY BOOK NEED TO BE?

Short answer:

10,000-20,000 words = PDF, Freebie, or short informational eBook.
40,000–60,000 words = This is pretty standard for a nonfiction book and is also regarded as a novella, not quite novel length, for fiction, especially if you want to publish conventionally.
60,000–100,000 words = This is on the long side for a nonfiction book and pretty standard for a novel.
100,000+ words = epic-length novel / academic book / biography. Careful when submitting anything any longer than this to a conventional publisher.

What people asking this question sometimes *really* mean:

If you are asking this question, you are trying to gage exactly how much work you are going to need to do. Be honest: seems like you're trying to motivate by talking yourself into completing the strict minimum. Writing a book is not just about writing a certain number of words, after which you are done. Your book needs to be complete, well-constructed, and impactful, and it will go through numerous rewrites and reworkings. If that sounds scary to you, you might want to examine your motivation. By asking this question, you are trying figure out what's worse: the pain, regret, and shame of never finishing your book, or the effort of writing one.

Question: How do I get published? How do I get an agent?

Short Answer:

In a nutshell, you have the choice between conventional publishing, self-publishing, or a hybrid service. In both cases, you can get all the information you need online. Read the fine print and make sure you follow all the requirements. In the case of conventional publishing, you will probably start with finding an agent (but only *after* you have a polished, complete manuscript). Writer's Digest is a valuable resource for finding an agent or a publisher. The literary agency's website will give you all the instructions and guidelines you need. The best way to get an agent and get published is to have a good, polished, sellable book and an author platform already in place.

What people asking this question sometimes *really* mean:

People who ask these questions want someone to tell them that the only work they need to do is to write their book. Once they have done that, the publishing thing will happen pretty much automatically. The hint to this way of thinking is in the language: they will "get" an agent and "get" published. Other than going to glamorous book signings, these writers hope that they will be able to ignore the rest of the process while their book magically goes on to become a bestseller. This is not the way the world works. The pain that this is revealing is actually the *imagined* pain of putting yourself out there, of promoting yourself, of feeling judged. It really stems from an inferiority complex brought on by ego. You think that if someone just held your hand it would be so much easier. This is what writing groups, writing buddies, and mentors are for. They will ease the pain of doing it all alone.

Question: Can you read/review/edit my story?

Short Answer:

No. Or, how much will you pay me?

What people asking this question sometimes *really* mean:

"Is there a shortcut or a cheaper way to do this? Can you share the load with me?"

If you're a friend, or someone in my writing group, or someone I interact with frequently online, and I have an interest in your genre or subject, of course I can at least take a look at it. If you're asking me this and I just met you (either in person or virtually), why haven't you found a real support group? Why won't you pay for a real editor? Probably because you actually are hoping you can do without the feedback. Some people complain to me that "they can't find readers" for their awesome story…which leads me to think that maybe it's not that awesome. If you jump all over people as soon as they give you feedback, that may also be a factor. Also, there are websites specifically for book reviews. Get on one of those, but you'll need to play by the rules. When you can't find readers or reviewers, or if those who read or review your work become swift enemies, look within. As for asking people to edit your book for free, just don't. Editing is a skill that people develop. Pay them for it. Or if you are strapped for cash, learn to be a good and fair editor, and do it on trade with other writers in the same situation. Your pain point is your fear of judgement, of taking a real risk, both to your ego and to your wallet.

Question: How can I find time to write?

Short Answer:

Cut out something else that is time consuming. (Social media, socializing, TV, cleaning the house…)

What people asking this question sometimes *really* mean:

"I can use my super busy life as the best excuse of all time, right?"

I don't know you, and I don't know your specific time constraints. If you're asking a stranger this general question, it's because you are looking for a ready-made excuse. Sorry, I won't give you one. If writing is important to you, you won't need to *find* the time, you will *make* the time. Even those of us with a full-time job and family obligations can steal away a moment here and there. Even short moments add up to lots of time eventually. You may not reach your goal of finishing your book as soon as you'd hoped, but you *will* finish it if it matters. The pain here is the fear that your ability or motivation isn't enough to warrant missing out on the other activities you will need to cast aside, at least temporarily, to make time for the writing and publishing process. And look, I get it. If you think it's hard to motivate to set time aside for telling a super fun and entertaining story, think of how hard it is to take time away from not only your busy life, but also your normal writing tasks, to write a hopefully not too dry non-fiction book…that's what I did here so believe me, when I tell you that you can make the time, you totally can.

Question: How do I [insert basic writing skill/task here]?

Short Answer:

Take a class. Look it up. Practice. Break it into manageable units. It's actually good that you realize what some of your specific shortcomings or areas of lesser skill are. Now fix them.

What people asking this question sometimes *really* mean:

"This writing thing is too hard, right? I don't know how to do the stuff, and not only do I not want to look it up, but I want someone to tell me how to do it, and if I even get to the point where I find someone to tell me how to do it, I'll forget what they said pretty fast, and my lack of knowledge will provide me with permission to stop."

You are displaying a major pain point: proof that maybe you aren't the best at something. You'll get over it. Good writers are not good because they are the best at writing dialogue, or because their grammar is perfect, or because they outline like a champ. They are good because they care about their story, and about how best to tell it.

Question: After how many rejections should I quit? How do I deal with rejection?

Short answer:

You should never quit. Rejection will never become fun or awesome. So just deal with it in whichever way works for you and move on.

What people asking this question sometimes *really* mean:

"When can I get permission to quit?"

Don't start out thinking about quitting. If your ultimate goal is to be a successful author, quitting just isn't part of the game plan. No roadmap to success has ever included quitting. It's simple: if you quit, you will never succeed. Now wait, I didn't say that you should keep beating a dead horse under the guise of "never quitting." No one ever said you couldn't pivot. How about instead of thinking of quitting, you think about coming back at whatever is failing from a different angle? Instead of quitting after a rejection, you could:

-Reflect

How did this make you feel? What can you do about it? Give yourself time to decide what your strategy should be.

-Rehash

Feel free to share a blow-by-blow account with a supportive friend or with an author who has been through it before. But don't revisit!

-Reevaluate

What are the reasons for my rejection? What can I improve upon? What are the shortcomings of my book?

-Regroup

Give yourself a little time to rest up, sharpen your skills, and think of a strategy.

-Reframe

Are you pursuing the correct outlets for your work? Are you within the correct genre or style? Is there another market where your work could do better?

-Resubmit

After the appropriate amount of time, after having put in the work to figure out how to improve upon your work, and after having drawn up a new list of agents who might be great advocates for your work, pitch again!

Should I use a pen name?

Short answer:

If you have a reason to use a pen name, sure. If you are a grade-school teacher writing BDSM or if you are super well-known for writing in another genre and don't want to confuse your fans, you can go ahead and use a pen name. If your parents were cruel and gave you a name that is a stupid pun, or if you have the same exact name as a famous author, yes, using a pen name is probably a smart idea. Otherwise, why?

What people asking this question sometimes *really* mean:

Some of you have fantasies of becoming so famous as an author that you couldn't possibly live a normal life if you used your real name. Honestly, the chances are pretty slim. Some of you have written revenge fantasies involving people you know and don't what the fallout that might come from publishing under their own name. This gets closer to what the real issue is. New writers feel that they can "hide" behind a pen name. Their ego won't be impacted as much by reviews, by success or lack thereof, because their identity is hidden. Also, they think that if they are writing under a pen name, they can't possibly be responsible for marketing their book, since they're anonymous. Wrong. There still needs to be a huge marketing effort, and you just made it harder with your demands for anonymity.

What should my cover look like? How do I get a good book cover?

Short answer:

Are you done or almost done with your book? No? Then it's too early to worry about that. And if you publish conventionally, someone else at the publishing job whose job it is to design book covers will do your cover and you'll have little to no input. If you self-publish, you will either buy a "pre-formatted" cover for cheap, or have a graphic designer make one for you. And then you'll have some input, but you should stick to something that is impactful, easy to read, and sets itself apart while remaining within the conventions of your genre.

What people asking this question sometimes *really* mean:

"I'm looking for a sticking point that will give me permission to quit or to focus on something other than writing my book." You lose yourself in little details and then you can pretend that, even though you didn't do any writing, you still moved forward on your book because you spend too much time thinking about the cover.

Years ago, a writer came into a writing group I was participating in and wanted the other writers to weigh in on her cover design. She'd gotten a painter friend to create something for her, and while the image was technically well painted, it was simply not a good cover.

"Oh wow, congrats! You finished your book," said one of the newbies to the group.

"No, I just started, but I wanted to get a jump on it," said the writer.

The organizer of the writing group looked puzzled. "I thought you were hoping to get this one conventionally published," he said.

"I do want that, but whichever publisher I'll go with needs to respect my creative vision," said the writer. "It's integral to the project."

Yikes. At that point, I knew not to touch that issue with a ten-foot pole. Almost all of the writers in the group quickly agreed that her proposed cover was simply perfect. I moved away and hence had to stop going to that writing group, but I am curious as to whether that writer ever finished and published her book, or whether she is still tied up in details that don't matter. My guess would be that someone told her the cover was all wrong, and she quit.

How do you make a living as a writer? How do you write a bestseller?

Short Answer:

You work at it all the time. You strategize your writing-related activities and the style and content of your book so that you have more chances of success. You make sure to write the best book possible, and you expand your definition of writing success so that it includes making money from writing-related activities such as editing, ghostwriting, or writing articles. You promote your work all the time. You market and advertise and keep your platform current. You constantly explore new avenues for your work.

What people asking these questions sometimes *really* mean:

"The odds of success are incredibly slim, right? Probably crazy to even start." People asking these questions want either a failproof formula that will be the perfect shortcut for them, sparing them time and effort, or they want an excuse to quit.

OK, all excuses aside, here are some examples of some very real holes in information that could possibly affect your ability to write a successful book:

-Basic education

First, something that you will hopefully find reassuring: you do not need to be a college graduate to write a great book. You do not need to have the best vocabulary or need to possess any kind of encyclopedic knowledge of anything specific at all. However, if you feel that you have serious deficits in knowledge that prevent you from writing a simple sentence or paragraph, let alone a book, you will want to start to figure out how to remedy the situation. Do you have a poor vocabulary, hesitation about how basic punctuation works, or a tenuous grasp of grammar? I am not one of those people who will try to reassure you by telling you that this is your editor's problem. No, it is obviously something that must addressed. However, it is not insurmountable. All you need to do is admit to yourself that this is the issue, and you can go about fixing it through courses, coaching, classes, and practice. Also, your education does not dictate the quality of the stories you have inside of you. Your motivation is going to need to come in strong to help you bridge the gap between ideas and expression, but it can be done!

-Not knowing how writing works within your genre

It is obvious that people are not born knowing how to write a book, or a script, or a presentation, or whatever... I don't mean to imply that you don't know how to put pen to paper and write sentences and paragraphs, but I mean that you are probably lacking crucial information about the specific building blocks that make up a work in your genre. This type of misinformation is most insidious because you can get pretty far in the writing process without realizing how much you do not know, and it will definitely get you stuck. Informing yourself on specific subjects such as how to write an outline, or how to write protagonists and antagonists (by the way, this even applies to non-fiction), or how to construct a plot structure will be a crucial step in avoiding the specific brand of frustration that comes from not knowing something, but not even knowing what exactly it is that you don't know.

Each style or genre has its rules, and you need to know them before you think of breaking any of them. You need to know simple things like format or style requirements, as in, don't write a 300,000-word novel and expect it to sell, or don't write a script without formatting it correctly...

Many of these holes in knowledge and information can be filled with reading. The more books or scripts in your genre you consume, the more you will gain an implicit sense of what makes a good work within that style. You will learn what does and does not work and be able to apply it to your own writing.

-Not knowing about the industry

Other information problems can stem from not knowing about the industry. If you don't know the first thing about the process of finishing and publishing a book, you may get almost to the end of the writing process, only to stop in your tracks because you don't know what to do next. If you do keep moving, it may be in the wrong direction, because of faulty assumptions about how the publishing world works. You may do yourself a disservice by skipping crucial steps such as editing, and this will severely impact your chances for success. Even for those who know that they need an editor, or who know that they might want to look for a literary agent, they may not know how to go about it, and will either end up wasting valuable time and money or freeze up and lose momentum. Your book will end up in a hidden folder in your computer, and that is the last thing we want to happen.

I know how bad this is because it happened to me. Years and years ago, I wrote a book without even giving a thought to how the publication process works. I had no idea that there was such a thing as literary agents, and once I had absorbed the information that they were out there and a crucial part of the conventional publishing process, I did not know what I should do to attract the attention of one. By this time, whipping my book into the kind of shape that was needed for conventional publication seemed like a huge task. Had I known all the steps and requirements from the get-go, it would have been so much easier.

A few years later, armed with somewhat more information, I did everything correctly, up to the writing of a kick-ass query letter. I pitched a bunch of agents, but was ignorant on what their responses meant, and on the fact that there would be many rejections, as well as many requests to read the rest of the manuscript, which would incur extra expenses for me and might not yield any positive results. After too many false hopes and high expectations, I was too impatient and unrealistic, and therefore let my motivation die too early.

Next, I decided that self-publishing was the way to go. Again, if I'd been a little more strategic about the process rather than doing everything on the fly and eventually running out of steam before my book could gain traction, I would have encountered more success.

Have I made lack of information sound like a huge problem? Well, it both is, and it isn't. It's a huge problem if you don't address it. It will block you every step of the way. But if you become aware of how much you don't know, you will be able to make up for this lack of knowledge in no time.

Do it strategically, though- don't fall into the trap of *"research-itis,"* where you obsessively over-research absolutely every detail, losing time and energy and confusing you more than anything else- this will lead to more writer's blocks. Sometimes too much information can be just as harmful as not enough, especially when various sources contradict each other, or when you fall into a rabbit hole on YouTube or on blogs. Some "writing coaches" out there are more concerned with having lots of content than with solving issues in a succinct and useful way, as they think this will make them more likely to be found on Google. You need to choose a source that delivers the key information in a manner that is accurate, to the point, and actionable.

You may also feel that you need more help than can be found in a single blog entry or short video. This is where online courses, writing groups, and mentorships come in. Again, make sure to choose wisely, and carefully consider the time and financial commitment. I am not here to recommend one over the other. This isn't that kind of book. Even though I offer a course and videos through Spalmorum, you need to search for what you feel in your heart and soul will work best for *you*, to propel you forward.

The bottom line is, don't get discouraged about how much you don't know- you are not alone, and the fact that you are conscious of any holes in expertise means you are already ahead of the game. Have you ever heard of the Dunning-Kruger effect? It is a piece of research out of Cornell University that proves that the most ignorant people have the tendency to feel most confident and even superior about their abilities. So, rest easy: if you think you're dumb, you're definitely not as dumb as you fear!

Again, mindset can play a huge role in information-based writer's block. A growth mindset goes a long way in letting you see information as something that can be gained when you need it.

Writer's block type 3: Lack of MOTIVATION

The third general type of writer's block, at least according to the Spalmorum Method, is motivation.

Things that sap motivation:

-Laziness/not taking the time

-Fear of failure/ego

-Solitude/working in a vacuum

I have met so many writers who have a great story in their head, but who find that they cannot make themselves take the time to write. Or they find a bit of time, start their project, and then shoot themselves in the foot because they fail to follow through. It is so much easier to talk about something and wish for something than it is to actually buckle down and do the work that is required for that thing to happen. But is it *really* easier? I think that it is really hard to be passionate about an idea and then to realize that you have not let that idea be born and shared with the world out of your own laziness.

Wait, that was an unfair jab, wasn't it? You're not just lazy.

It's just really hard to find motivation when you are working in a vacuum. Writing is one of the most solitary activities there is.

It is also really hard work and it has an uncertain outcome. Your brain tricks you into giving up too early because it has learned that the chances of your book being a success are slim. You know what, though? The chances of success are *way* higher if you actually finish your book, and then put in the work to whip it into shape and go through the necessary steps to get it in front of readers.

Wouldn't it be so much easier and more motivating if you had help? A friend to cheer you on and encourage you? That, my friend, is called a writing group. I host one in Marin County each Wednesday afternoon. Some of my writers were reticent at first. They were scared. They didn't know if they could write a book. They didn't know if the other writers would be supportive. Little by little, I've seen them blossom. Every single time we meet, one or more of them blows me away. If you're not in a writing group, I highly encourage you to join one. Every excuse you make to *not* join one: geography, no time, etc. does not truly hold up, because if you can find time to watch TV or YouTube or play video games, and if you live within 50 miles of any kind of civilization, you can find a writing group, or start a writing group, and that will be one of the best things you ever did for your writing career. But I know the real reason many writers don't do it, especially the writers who suffer most from writer's block: They're scared.

Come on, be honest with yourself: are you scared? If so, you're not alone. Interestingly, only a small minority of writers take advantage of the valuable tool that is writing groups. Writers who are suffering from writer's block do not want to expose themselves. They're afraid of being judged, of being compared to others, and of measuring up on some meaningless level.

Change your mindset now: see other writers as allies rather than enemies. Friends enrich your life in many ways, and author friends can share vital tools with you, and serve to motivate, inspire, and educate. They truly alleviate many of the pain points inherent in writing, but only if you let them. I have seen so many writers get caught up in the "competitive" aspect of writers' groups, especially critique-based writer's groups where the moderator has not set up the expectations of what critiques should and shouldn't be. This can cause authors pain and frustration rather than the joy and excitement that they could have through participating in a supportive group.

A Yale study found that many writers would like motivational help, but that it would have to be anonymous. In light of what I have just laid out, that makes sense- it's so much easier to hide behind your computer keyboard, definitely a comfort zone for most writers even, if it is sometimes the very object that represents your frustration. But instead of writing, you get lost in endless chat rooms, articles, and reviews. This actually can make you feel worse rather than better. There is such a thing as seeking too much reassurance, and you need to keep away from that pitfall.

Believe me, I'm not just lecturing to you: *I've been there*. I feel that I'd read so many articles about writers block before I even finished my first novel that I could literally have written a book about it way back then- I certainly had done my research... but it's actually a good thing that I waited. First of all, writing novels was my priority and I'm glad that I kept it that way enough to eventually finish and publish them, even if I made crucial mistakes. It's a wonder I finished them at all. Back then, I was still stuck in a self-defeating cycle of motivational writer's block brought on by my ego. I saw other writers as competition, thought that my ideas might get "stolen" by another writer or screenwriter, and jealously guarded everything I did. I released books under pen names so family and friends and professional contacts wouldn't judge me.

I've mentioned that motivation also can be lacking when you see your chances of success as slim. Looking at facts and figures about the book industry, it's easy to rationalize the impossibility of ever publishing a book by looking at the percentage of books that get finished, the percentage of books that get published, and the relatively small number of books that get sold. You've heard that even libraries no longer have room for a fraction of the books that get published each year... and let's not even talk about the ever-disappearing independent bookstore.

But truly, for all of the external blocks to success, you must realize that the numbers are not as bad as they look: if you do 100% of the work needed to get your book written as well as possible and out on the market with a solid sales and marketing strategy, your chances of success are exponentially stronger. There are a relatively small number of new writers who make it. But you *can* be one of those if you play your cards right and do that consistently.

The only 100% certitude is that if you don't finish and promote your book, you will not succeed.

Many wannabe writers ask: How can I make a living from my writing? This is a lot of pressure to put on something that you are relatively new to. Unfortunately, this is also something that many creatives fall prey to, too early in the process: the pressure to monetize. Imagine if you had just learned to use QuickBooks and now you were putting pressure on yourself to become a successful tax accountant, with a specific salary to boot. Imagine if you decided that you would only take up knitting if you knew you could sell your handiwork and live off of the proceeds from the get-go. Sounds ridiculous, right?

There *are* ways to make a living from writing, but most of the time it means you will have to do something writing-related, but not necessarily related to your latest book: teaching, journalism, copywriting, editing, ghostwriting…the list goes on. If financial gain is your only benchmark of success, I would probably keep writing as a hobby and work on building a different career where the chances of significant financial gain are more built-in. There is no guarantee that your book will become a best-seller and make you a millionaire, but conversely, if you don't finish your book at all, I can guarantee that the chances of it happening go down to zero.

Later in this book, there is a section that lays out the closest thing to a formula for writing a best-seller. I know that having some chance of success is definitely a motivator. One of the ingredients of a bestseller is purpose. Purpose comes from knowing what motivates you. So, let's take a moment to figure out your motivations. Each set of motivations can lead to a different type of writer's block, for which we can then give you more targeted solutions.

What is important to you? What are your motivations? If you understand your motivations, it can give you ammunition to eliminate potential pain points that can arise if you get stuck.

Key Questions to ask yourself before starting to write a book

Why do I want to be a writer?

Asking why you want to be a writer may be too general a question, so the question is instead: why do you want to write *this* book? Do you want to entertain readers with a great story? Inspire them? Make them laugh? Make them cry? Make a million dollars? Prove something? You can see how this question is really important. Whatever your goals are with this book, you are going to need to work on those in addition to the simpler goal of finishing a book. Just know that ahead of time, because it is possible that you may get stuck along the way because of the perceived or anticipated pain of not reaching that specific goal.

Do I want to make money with this?

To expand on the "make a million dollars" thing in the previous question: seriously, do you ideally want to make money with your book, or do you not care? This will affect a lot of elements, from subject matter and style to format. If you know that you will experience the pain of disappointment or feel that the whole exercise of writing a book was futile, which elicits the pain of thinking you wasted your precious time, imagine that pain and lean into it: there are certain steps you will need to take to make the likelihood of making money higher.

How hard is this going to be?

How much research will you have to do to write your book, and do you currently have the skills and knowledge to see it through? It's better to figure out early how much work you need to do to "level up" rather than experience the pain and embarrassment of feeling stupid or incapable after you succumb to an information block.

Who is my reader?

Who is your ideal audience, and how will you reach them? Yep, this is Marketing 101, and as a writer, it may not be one of your core competencies, but if you want to avoid the pain of launching a book to crickets, you do need a plan and a strategy. If you don't want to put time and effort into promotion, just know that you will be ever so much less likely to reach that dream audience. Make that pretty darn unlikely.

How will I publish?

Is the goal to get a traditional publishing deal, or do you just want to get your book "out there" more quickly by going the self-publishing route? Keep in mind that any shortcuts you take can and will affect your success. There are a lot of "in-between" hybrid options as well these days that you might want to explore. If your goal is a traditional publishing deal, make sure you know *why* you want that, and educate yourself as to what it entails. Make sure you're clear on this. So many authors (including me) have an idealized view of how we want to publish, and if that falls through, we experience the pain of failure even if we end up publishing another way. The majority of writers who fail at publishing in their chosen manner, however, will probably just experience the pain of giving up.

How much is this going to cost?

Do you have a budget in place for your book? Even if you go with a traditional publisher, you will need, at the very least, to pay for an editor and an attorney. If you self-publish, you will need even more time with an editor, as well as a cover designer, layout specialist, tech, and marketing/advertising. Make a budget. Try to determine the point where the pain of spending money is balanced by the knowledge that you need to invest in yourself in order to succeed. The pain of paying good money actually makes it more likely that you will motivate and follow through. This is why people are more likely to finish and act on an online course that cost them more rather than a free seminar. This is why people pay for a personal trainer or for Weight Watchers. The support is just a part of the success equation. Paying for it makes it feel more important. So, use the money you spend to motivate you more. Spending money on something that is of value to you hurts way less than wasting money on something you never followed through with.

Am I motivated enough?

How will you feel if you don't start or finish writing this book? This sound like a stupid question, but seriously, really imagine the worst-case scenario: you, about to die, that book still just in your head, everyone around you thinking, "yep, I knew they wouldn't write it!" How does that make you feel? Whether your answer is, "I *must* finish this book!" or "Meh," that is going to tell you a lot.

This question makes you pinpoint the pain level involved with your block. No pain, no gain. So, if your answer is a real, sincere "meh," maybe you really should find another creative outlet that feeds your soul and stop complaining about writer's block. But…if you really didn't care, you wouldn't have picked up this book, or it wouldn't have been recommended to you. When you don't care about whether you succeed at all, or even to what degree you will succeed, there is theoretically zero pain involved, and hence zero reason for you to do that thing. The good news is that you have not wasted time or money with this book. If it isn't writing, think of something else that you care about and that you are blocked in. Writers, there may be another thing that pops into your head at this point as well- a second or even a third passion project that you have in mind. You're going to need to prioritize, but the mindset changes in this book with help you with that other project as well in the long run.

Can I see my end goal?

How do you think you will feel when the book is finished? What will you do to celebrate its' launch? This is where you get to forget about all the potential pain points and think about pleasure for once! Imagine your ideal life when you have achieved your goal of being an author, as you keep pursuing new writing goals and achievements. Pretty wonderful, right?

Are you starting to find your motivation, or starting to see pain points where your motivation needs a little boost? Good.

Whenever you are lacking in motivation, imagine the worst-case scenario, the one where you let that lag in motivation convince you to not finish your work.

Now really lean into the painfulness of that result. Pile pain on top of pain. Really beat yourself up.

Here is an example:

-I didn't finish my book.
-I had told my friends I was going to finally write it and now they know I don't follow through.
-I wasted the money I spent on that new laptop I bought expressly to finish my book.
-I spent a bunch of hours writing, and I'll never get them back.
-My parents are disappointed that their kid didn't amount to anything.
-I'm less of a role model to my kids than I should be.
-That insufferable guy in my writing group is going to publish a book, and I'm not.
-I can't even keep promises to myself. Wow.
-Damn I'm lazy and unmotivated. Who knew I was this bad? Actually, now, everyone does.
-Guess I actually don't have a real purpose in life.

Ouch, right?

Now make that pain convince you to act.

Chapter 3: Ego Block- Is your ego's fear of rejection blocking you?

Yes, Ego block gets its own chapter. Not because the ego is so special. I gave it its own chapter because it doesn't play well with others, and because it tends to contaminate so much of the writing process.

Ego should have as little as possible to do with the writing process. We should instead focus on maintaining a healthy mindset, which leads to action, to relentlessly move forward and do our best work, to fulfill our purpose as authors.

"We tend to think, or at least fear, that creative dreams are egotistical... This thinking must be undone." -Creativity teacher and writer Julia Cameron

Right on, Julia! Feeling that creative dreams are egotistical creates a fundamental shame around our creative output. It is what makes it so much harder to promote artistic efforts than it is to promote another product that is less personal, such as a new kind of toothbrush or revolutionary kitty litter.

Not all artists are automatically egomaniacs. That is not the nature of creativity. Not all writers are raging narcissists, obsessed with their own words and ideas. I find that it is actually quite the opposite in general: writers care about sharing ideas and stories and making connections. They are fundamentally generous. But sometimes, they go about everything the wrong way, and their ego trips them up.

Don't you need a huge ego to believe that your ideas are so important that you should spend so much time and energy on trying to get them out into the public? Well, you do need a healthy ego in some ways, but you also need to keep it in check. You see, ego is where the majority of so-called writer's blocks come from. The thoughts that are fueled by your ego create fear. We become blocked because we fear that others will judge our production and threaten the self-image that our ego has built up for us.

Simply writing feels like a very vulnerable act. But you're not *actually* being vulnerable if what you write stays in your computer, or even worse, if your idea simply stays in your head. Yes, it's pretty scary when you are confronted by your inadequate words on the page or the screen, and I know that the really terrifying part comes next: when someone else sees your words. They're basically reading your thoughts and judging them. Creative fields are pretty unique in this way. Our creative production feels so very personal. Be honest with yourself: you've worried about exposing your innermost thoughts to others at some point, or all the time, haven't you?

What is ego?

In a nutshell, ego is the persona, the avatar we all create for ourselves. It's the idealized version of us: good looking, cool, successful, talented, popular, and wealthy, or any combination of those. The ego is what we get when we combine all of our beliefs about our personality, talents, and abilities. Sounds like how we form a mindset, doesn't it? Yes, it does, and it is even more powerful than a simple mindset when you let it be. And make no mistake: the more you let your ego drive you, the more pain you end up feeling.

Why does letting your ego rule you create pain? Because anything that proves your self- image false creates a *cognitive dissonance*: the painful sense that what we believe to be true, is not actually true. Most of us will do anything to avoid this. And the worst part is, we do it so naturally, so automatically, that usually we don't even notice that we are doing it. Unfortunately, this has extremely negative effects on our writing career.

When you hear someone say that someone else "has a big ego," they usually mean that the person has a bit of a superiority complex that can be reflected in an arrogant affect. Yet the arrogance is truly just on the surface. Having a huge ego more often causes low self-esteem or at the very least elevated self-doubt. True confidence, on the other hand, does not stem from ego. Confidence comes from a healthy attitude regarding your skills, abilities, and experience. Being self-accepting and realistic about yourself can help to bolster your confidence, as can allowing yourself to be vulnerable. But your ego won't let you put yourself in a position of vulnerability, because it perceives this as a potentially dangerous weakness.

Go on any author chat room and you will see the ugly behaviors that authors with huge egos engage in when the anonymity afforded by online communication gives their ego permission to impact their behavior unfettered. These are the people mocking, policing, lecturing, and sometimes doing so much worse. Imagine the inner pain that would cause that kind of acting out. That is the result of giving in to your ego.

How can you tell whether your ego is impacting you in the realm of writing? Notice the emotional reactions you have to other writers' success, to critiques, to feeling insecure at a writing event or in writing group, to not even wanting to participate in writing groups for fear of leaving yourself exposed and judged. Hey, don't worry- we all do it. The key is to become more conscious of what is going on so that we can fix it.

Do any of these behaviors sound familiar? Have you ever engaged in any of these behaviors?

Playing the Victim

With this mindset, everything that happens to you, every setback, every failure, every challenge, is not your fault. In your opinion, people should be treating you better and giving you the recognition you deserve instead of creating obstacles for your success. Putting yourself in this victim mentality may absolve you (in head) of the responsibility for your own failures, but it also means that you are giving up control, and this does not bode well for your writing success.

Here's a story for you: I was catching up with a writer I know while taking a hike. She was angrily relating how furious she was that a certain literary magazine hadn't published one of her short stories despite the fact that one of the editors was an acquaintance of hers. She focused on how the editor had let her down and had given her a stupid excuse for why they hadn't run the story. Curious, I asked what the excuse was.

"She said I missed the publication deadline by a single day," she said. "Ridiculous! I gave her a piece of my mind and then she blocked me on Facebook!"

I was truly taken aback by how my friend's ego could blind her so completely that she might think that a literary magazine should wait on her to print their publication, and that it was reprehensible that they hadn't. At this point I had to change the subject because there was such a huge disconnect between reality and what her ego was telling her. Had my friend simply apologized and acted professionally when handing in her late work, she would have had at least a chance at seeing it in print. Instead, her ego had made her burn a bridge.

Defending "your" turf

I mentioned this earlier: some writers aggressively defend "their" turf, as though there is a limited amount of writing success to go around, and that someone else succeeding will impact their own success. These are the same writers who troll others online or leave unnecessarily negative critiques and reviews. These authors feel personally attacked if another writer gains accolades or attention, and it is frankly energy badly spent.

A writer in one of the writing groups I attended in LA was telling me how she felt upset that one of her friends had gotten a writing job on a sitcom. "I went to a cocktail party and everyone was congratulating her," she said. "It really hurt my feelings." As she spoke, I furtively scanned the room, hoping for her sake that there were no other writers within earshot. Your negativity does not make you shine. It makes you look bad. Even worse, worrying about your failures all the time makes you more focused on failure than success. It's like a self-fulfilling prophecy.

Getting easily offended

The ego can lead you to believe that absolutely everything is a personal attack. Someone can mention a theory of writing that does not align with yours or claim to prefer a genre other than your own, and you feel that they are directly questioning your abilities, talents, and judgement. You will twist general statements into perceived insults. You will take your editor's helpful comments badly. Again, this is a waste of time and energy. This will lead to a breakdown in the writing and promotional process of your book. Editors, publishers, and possible outlets for your work will not want to associate with you. Publishing is a business. People are trying to make money. Do not take these things personally. Instead, try to make your book more sellable.

Self-imposed solitude

Your belief that success is the main objective and that you must "beat" others to it makes you see other writers as competition. You become protective of your status and of your ideas, and generally insufferable to others. I was mentioning to a friend that I hadn't seen or heard from one of our mutual friends, a fellow writer, in a while. "She doesn't go out much anymore," I was told. "She says she can't stand the negativity and doesn't need the distractions." Apparently, she had told my friend in a previous conversation that anyone who doesn't feel that way is not a real writer.

Solitude is of course a crucial ingredient for writers, but we all need balance. Going out into the world feeds our hearts, our souls, and our creativity, and helps us to make crucial connections. Don't skip it out of fear and ego.

Constantly searching for validation

You torture your friends with demands for compliments and positive reviews. You seek out awards that will prove to everyone that you are the best there is. Whenever someone asks for a book recommendation in your presence, you are livid if your friends don't immediately suggest yours. Just because someone compliments you or gives you an award doesn't mean you're better. Isn't it better to work hard and do everything you can possibly do so that your book genuinely touches people? In that case, the accolades will come organically.

Comparing

Your ego wants to help you maintain the belief that you are better, more special, and more deserving than others. At first you try to put on blinders: you avoid writing groups, where you may be confronted with another writer's talent. You stop reading glowing book reviews. Hell, you may stop reading books. But it's human nature: you can't help but take a peek at what others are up to. Unfortunately, you will sometimes notice that these others are not half bad. This starts to make you feel inferior. If you feel that someone else is more talented, you let it destroy your mood. To compensate, you look for faults everywhere possible. You put other writers down, either in your head or out loud. Should anyone have the gall to put you down in turn, whether it's a fellow writer or a reader who didn't love your book, you insult them because they just don't "get you."

Comparing never leads to anything good. There is always someone out there who is better than you. Always. And yes, there will be writers who are worse. Forget brilliance and fame, and focus on good storytelling and your audience, and you'll be better and happier.

Fear of judgement

Here's another reason you don't join a writing group, another reason you probably don't want an editor, who may tell you what's wrong with your book. It's also why you don't put yourself out there or ever write anything weird or deep, or different from what is expected of you. You stick to whatever has worked for you in the past. Sometimes that past is really, really far back. Fear of judgement truly keeps you from growing as a writer. It prevents you from being vulnerable. It stands between you and your audience, preventing you from connecting with them in any way that's real or raw. If you can't escape your ego's fear of judgement (and by the way, I am absolutely not judging you if that's the case- it's really, really hard sometimes), maybe you *should* use a pen name. You'll still need to market this pen name identity in all of the ways you would market a real person- it may even be trickier to do. So don't make that decision rashly.

Letting fear of rejection keep you from achievement

Your belief that rejection is the worst leads you to do anything to avoid rejection, including never actually finishing anything, so that there is zero chance that it could be rejected. Is rejection really the worst thing that could happen? Isn't it possible to survive rejection? Even more incredible, is it possible to thrive after rejection?

1.   John Grisham's first novel was rejected 25 times. He has since published 40 novels and has sold more than 275 million books to date. He splits his time between at least 3 luxury homes.

2.   *Chicken Soup for the Soul* received 134 rejections. It was eventually printed by a tiny publishing house in Florida but did so well that it laid the foundations for an empire. Jack Canfield and Mark Victor Hansen eventually sold the company (I'm guessing for a big pile of cash) and seem to be doing pretty well for themselves other than maybe having to juggle so many paid speaking engagements.

3.   Beatrix Potter couldn't find a publisher for *The Tale of Peter Rabbit*, so she initially self-published it. Seems to have worked out ok for her in the end.

4.   Stephen King's *Carrie* was rejected dozens of times. It was his fourth novel, but the first to be published, and he almost didn't continue writing past the first few pages. Thankfully, his wife fished it out of the trash and persuaded him that it wasn't the absolute crap he thought it was. King is also known for writing under several pseudonyms as a test for whether he could recreate his initial success. Spoiler alert: he couldn't, but his other books still didn't do half bad, considering.

5.   *Moby*-Dick was rejected multiple times. Peter J. Bentley of Bentley & Son Publishing House wrote: "First, we must ask, does it have to be a whale? While this is a rather delightful, if somewhat esoteric, plot device, we recommend an antagonist with a more popular visage among the younger readers. For instance, could not the Captain be struggling with a depravity towards young, perhaps voluptuous, maidens?"

When it was published, Melville had to pay for the typesetting and plating himself. Still, readers seemed to like the book.

6.   One of Hemingway's rejections for *The Sun Also Rises* read: "If I may be frank — you certainly are in your prose — I found your efforts to be both tedious and offensive. You really are a man's man, aren't you? I wouldn't be surprised to hear that you had penned this entire story locked up at the club, ink in one hand, brandy in the other. Your bombastic, dipsomaniac, where-to-now characters had me reaching for my own glass of brandy." Actually seems pretty accurate but Hemingway still did all right as a writer.

7.   When Rudyard Kipling pitched a story to the *San Francisco Examiner*, he received this response: "...you just don't know how to use the English language." In 1907, he was awarded the Nobel Prize for Literature.

Getting rejected by the gatekeepers is always a difficult blow, but it does get easier. Also, getting your ego knocked down a few notches can be a good thing. Just don't let it keep you from your purpose.

Why is the intense pain of a blow to your ego a good thing?

In reality, letting your ego control you is not a confidence booster at all. It prevents you from having a true and honest connection to the world. Truth and honesty are essential for good writing. The ego disconnects you from this truth and from the other people that can be an inspiration and a supportive community for you. By getting too wrapped up in yourself, you can lose touch with your audience and with everything else.

English academic Toby Litt sums it up brilliantly: "Bad writing is almost always a love poem addressed by the self to the self. The person who will admire it first and last and most is the writer herself. While bad writers may read a great many diverse works of fiction, they are unable or unwilling to perceive the things these works do which their own writing fails to do."

Hopefully, you can learn to funnel the pain of a blow to your ego into strength and determination, to (even briefly) move aside the curtain of denial that stands between your work and objectivity.

Has your ego has taken an overly large space in your psyche?

Try to reestablish the balance by actively doing the things that your ego makes so much more difficult:

-Encouraging others and promoting their ideas and talents

-Engaging in radical self-awareness

-Toning down your need for recognition and redefining success

-Mentoring others

-Sharing ideas and advice

-Becoming a more active member of the writing community

Without silencing ego, you will come across blocks all across all *six* steps of the writing process.

What? Six steps? If you were paying attention before, you may recall that I had mentioned three steps for writing a book. Well, now you can handle more of the truth. Read on.

Chapter 4: The "Lost pieces" of the writer's block puzzle.

Many experts on the writing process agree that there are six steps to writing. Yes, there are a full six phases in the writing process, whether we are talking about fiction, memoir, or nonfiction. Most books about writer's block, as I have said before, speak mostly of the inspiration block that affects only part of the writing process, this part being the "writing part" of your book. However, it is the "bookends" of this writing process that determine your ultimate success. You may not be surprised at this point to find that it is in these "bookend" sections, the beginning and the end of the writing process, where most writers fail. What are the six steps of the writing process? They are:

1) Pre-writing:

Pre-writing is where doubt first makes an appearance. This is the step where you're trying to psych yourself up to believe you can do this whole writing thing. This is where writers struggle with the idea of being an imposter, where they fear that the impossibility of success means that they shouldn't even try, and where they doubt that any of their ideas will actually make a good book. All writers entertain these thoughts at some juncture. You have, or you will. I've finally learned to push through this harmful way of thinking with an adjusted mindset and believe that you will learn to reframe these thoughts as well after finishing this book.

Two of the most crucial parts of this pre-writing process are finding your "why" as an author and finding the "why" of the story you want to tell. This in turn will help you to figure out the best way to tell that story, in terms of genre, format, style, characters, location, and more. If you want to be successful, you must be crystal clear on your intentions, your goals, and your plan. This means that you need to know who your end reader is. This means figuring out who your ideal audience is, and how to best reach them, whether in stylistics of the book itself, or with your author platform. You need to know what you want to do with the story. This is an absolutely non-negotiable part of the process. People who jump into writing a book with no plan and no intention will ultimately fail. If you find an exception, know that it is just that: an exception to a well-established rule.

In this phase:

-Do your research: read things in your genre, things written by authors who seem to have a reader base like the one you hope to attract.

-Start to check in with yourself, to determine whether you are lacking any of the skills you need to get this done. Start to figure out how to get those skills.

-Start to build your author platform.

-Try to commit to a writing schedule and writing spot(s) that will work for you.

-Create a location and character bible with all of the details your need to keep straight when you are describing your book's uniquely complex world.

Yes, this is already a lot of work and we haven't even gotten to the "real" writing part yet.

Approximately only 5% of the people who claim they want to write a book even make it all the way through this first step.

2) Writing:

Many experts include outlining in the pre-writing step, but I prefer to put it in this step. During this section of the writing process, you will make a quick outline and then start fleshing it out with the details, the interactions between characters, the scenes that are playing out in your head.

You shouldn't let your ego play tricks on you during the section, and of course some people will. But suffice it to say that if you go back over your mantras and do any of the exercises we recommended earlier in the book, you should be doing fine with this step. keep in mind that this is a very rough first draft. Carry on despite inspiration block. Don't think about things such as word count or grammar, don't worry about what comes next, just try to get your story down and write down what's important. This step is key, obviously. It's what most people imagine when they think of "writing a book," and it's hard enough to get through without having to make it harder on yourself with your perfectionism.

Of the people who completed the pre-writing step, only about 5% get all the way through this writing phase.

3) Revision:

Revision is the part where it is completely fine to be a little bit critical of what you have created. This is where you are doing a self-edit, and you are examining your story for logic, readability, pacing, details, character arc… all of the big pieces that make a huge difference in how your story comes through. Some of the crucial things to address in this stage is making sure that you have the correct word count. Be realistic about how long your book is. Too short or too long will impact your chances of publication and of finding readers. Make sure that you include all of the information you need, with none of the superfluous repetition. Look at the flow and the pacing of the story. Does everything happen in the correct order, is there a sense of building of tension throughout, do the characters undergo a character arc. Now, look at removing some things. Is there a superfluous character? Does the action move around to unnecessary locations? Is there any confusion created by too many details that do not really contribute to the story? Also, is there any superfluous backstory? This section is where many writers run into trouble because they don't want to delete sections they worked so hard on. Try to see your story through the eyes of a stranger. Be as dispassionate as you can.

This is where you're expected to do that terrible thing writers and editors call "kill your darlings." What does this mean? It means get rid of all that stuff you really like and had so much fun writing:

-The detailed description of a meal your characters enjoyed, during which absolutely nothing happened.

-The long interlude in which we get a rundown of your character's entire wardrobe, each outfit dissected down to its last pearl button.

-The character who is utterly charming and witty, but who is the literary equivalent that shallow friend you keep inviting out even though they truly don't have much to contribute beyond their good looks and the occasional joke.

If it makes you feel any better, you can save all of these things in a separate file, to be used later. Spoiler alert: you won't use them later.

Quite a few more would-be authors give up at this point.

4) Editing:

This step is a long process, and you need to do yourself a favor of giving at the time and attention it deserves. You can and of course should do a large part of the editing yourself, especially if that is one of your strengths, but you also absolutely always will need an outside view, preferably a professional one, of your work. A talented editor will attempt to make 100% sure that there are no problems with grammar, spelling, and punctuation, they will check your manuscript for clarity and structure, and they will basically ensure that the all-important readability of your book is everything that it can be.

In this stage, the ego can rear its ugly head, and some authors truly detest any kind of feedback, even if it is from a professional editor. It is so important to take any editorial advice seriously, but with a grain of salt. At the end of the day, you know your story best, but you need to be fully honest with yourself and with your work when you decide to ignore select pieces of the editor's advice. I know so many writers who actually never get to this stage because they have resistance against subjecting their work to any kind of correction, and/or they also do not want to spend the money. Their fear and pain of rejection holds them back. At this stage, the reality of publication is coming closer and closer.

The vast majority of writers never make it to this point. However, this is still not the hardest part.

5) Publishing:

Here is another stage where many more writers will fall through the cracks or will give up. Those who are seeking traditional representation and publication may balk at the difficulty of formulating a query letter. They may shoot themselves in the foot by not following submission guidelines, and they may give up at the first sign of rejection. Understanding that rejection happens to everyone is crucial here.

Some authors decide to go to the self-publishing route, and this also presents a host of difficulties. The large number of small decisions that must be made when self-publishing, including formatting, cover, getting an ISBN, negotiating the upload, and setting up various author profiles, scares off more than one author. This is the point at which technology starts to play a part, and many writers will employ the excuse that they are not technologically oriented as a reason to quit. Think about this: doesn't it makes no sense, when you've put in an incredible amount of work, more than 95% of other would-be writers, to give up now? So close to the finish line? Isn't that going to be even more painful than never having started at all? Yet so many writers do exactly that. I have, and it isn't pretty. The great news is that if you've done this as well, you may be well ahead of the game: dust off that manuscript, give it another edit, and get cracking on publishing it!

6) Marketing:

Aaaaahhh, here we are, the last part!

Except it's not truly the last part because you should have been doing it all along. Also, this part is never finished. It's probably the most problematic part of the writing process, for almost every single writer. In fact, many of the writers who never actually got to this stage probably did not get to the stage partially out of fear of having to deal with it.

Marketing a book is hard. Marketing yourself is uncomfortable. Self-promotion brings out the trolls, tests your strength, your patience, and your resilience, and can break even the strongest one among us. So many writers shoot themselves in the foot because they refused to do their own marketing. While I was doing research for this book, I noticed a ton of people asking whether they "actually need" to market themselves. Writers in my writing group will ask me the same question multiple times, as if the answer is going to miraculously change. The fact that writers are asking this question in that form means that they hope that the answer is *no*. No matter what anyone says, the answer is always *yes*.

You need to market yourself. There is no magic that will cause your book to get discovered without you putting it out there, and without you putting yourself out there as an author. There is no publishing company that will take a chance on an inexperienced author with zero platform and zero desire to build one.

Here is the fundamental truth that you must remember when it comes to marketing. I know that marketing is literally a pain. I know that self-promotion is inherently painful. But you must get yourself to a place where you firmly believe that the pain of not having your book dreams come true is worse than the pain and embarrassment and blows to your ego that will happen with self-promotion. I'm not going to sugarcoat it. There are uncomfortable moments every single day in an author's life, and many of these uncomfortable moments are at the hands of online trolls or critics. But when your sense of self and your sense of purpose are strong enough, you will know that the pain of never fulfilling your purpose makes that's stuff look like child's play.

Here are a few of the excuses that I've heard from the writers in my writing group or online. I'm going to address each one individually, because I do take this pain point very seriously. It is so important for you to understand that you are not alone in your reticence to self-market, but self-promotion is crucial for your success.

Marketing/selling excuses:

-I'm a writer, not a marketer."

If you want to be an author, you will also need to be a marketer. It's part of the job description. You can absolutely be an *aspiring writer* and never be a marketer, but you will never be a successful author without being a marketer. Marketing is a nonnegotiable piece of the success equation. You cannot hire someone to do 100% of this for you, because what your readers are looking for is a connection with you, and you cannot farm that out. Authenticity and an author's voice are very difficult to fake, and the big question is, why would you want to do that to your readers? If you know upfront that you are not a natural marketer, it is your job to start becoming one. Not later. Now. Trying to convince yourself that it is acceptable not to be a marketer is just a form of resistance, one of the manifestations of writer's block that will prevent you from any form of success.

-I tried everything and it didn't work.

This excuse is funny. You clearly did not try everything. You didn't even try *part* of everything. In fact, you probably made some kind of half-assed attempt at doing things, and you did them wrong, and now you are going to use it as an excuse to never do any of the things you need to do.

If your marketing did not work at all, that's because you were not doing it right. Find out how to do it right, and then actually do it. Once you have found out what works, you must also realize that you're going to need to be doing it for a while, because it takes time for anything to gain traction.

Many of us are guilty of ascribing to a form of magical thinking that tells us that if we simply put our work out into the world, people will discover it and we will see swift success.

This never happens. You need to put it out into the world, and then promote, promote, promote.

Recognition takes repetition. Your potential readers need to see your posts come across their feed or come across their consciousness multiple times before they even register that you exist. It takes a long time to convert someone from a stranger to a reader, and then from a reader to a fan.

If what you tried before didn't work, that doesn't mean you should just quit. That's crazy! When you were learning to ride a bike, did you just decide that since it didn't work on the first try, you would never try riding a bike ever again? It's a ludicrous argument! No, you got back on that bike and came at it differently until you learned to balance, and learned to pedal while balancing, and then it became second nature. Objectively, even though marketing is psychologically taxing, it is technically one of the easier parts of the whole writing process. If you get over your ego and become radically honest with yourself, you will realize this, and you will stop saying that you've tried everything.

One caveat: not to discourage you, but unlike riding a bike, sometimes, when it comes to promoting a book, things will work for a while and then stop working as well. That's when you will need to use your imagination, research abilities, and resilience to come up with a new plan. To continue with the bike analogy, by this point you'll have gained momentum, so you'll still be moving forward, and you'll be less likely to fall off, even if the bike has gotten old. You may be reluctant to buy a shiny new bike with all the bells and whistles. But you should. You deserve the new bike. The learning curve won't be as steep, and before long you'll find yourself going faster than you ever thought possible. Ok. Bike analogy over.

-I'm too late in the game for building a platform.

You are too late in the game to be the king or queen of MySpace, sure. You might be too late in the game to be killing it on Snapchat or on TikTok with all the cool kids. But there are people out there who are still amassing huge followings on YouTube, Facebook, Instagram, and Quora, and they are relative newcomers. They simply produce high-quality content that inspires people, and they stay consistent, and they keep working at it, and promoting it. Preemptively deciding that you're too late in the game for self-promotion is not a logical argument. If you're too late in the game for a certain form of platform, or a certain corner of the Internet, be early in the game for something else. The ways of marketing oneself are not as limited as you're making it sound. You're a writer, you have a great imagination. Now use it. The truth is that people are always looking for content. People thrive on novelty. That is your advantage as a creative.

-I'm not good at technology.

I'm great at technology. I was born great at it. As a baby, I knew how to program and code without anyone telling me how. I was born knowing how to build a website, and how to do graphic design. Incredible, right? It's also not true.

No one is born being good at technology and computer-related stuff. No one knows how to do any of the many things you need to do to promote yourself without first figuring it out. You know what successful people do? They learn how to do things. Learning how to do things is part of the author's job description as well. If you don't want to learn to do the things, the second-best option is paying someone to do the things.

Paying someone to promote you straight off the bat is truly a distant second to starting off with doing it yourself. I am not saying that you shouldn't consider hiring a social media manager once you are bringing in an income for your writing, or that you can't hire someone to build your website if you are super stressed out by it and truly feel incapable of building even the simplest plug-and-play site ever.

You just need to weigh in the fact that it will cost you in many ways:

-You will literally pay for it. Is it in your budget, or will it make you cheap out on things you need even more, such as editing?

-You will have less control over what gets posted, how your website looks, and all of that good stuff. You may need to update something quickly and not know how, or not have the right password, or have to pay extra to have it done.

-You will not build an organic rapport with potential readers. Many services that promise to grow your social media accounts do so with unsavory "follow-unfollow" methods.

-Most people do whatever they can to cut out the middleman, not add one.

These simple facts alone have kept me current on technology, just enough to know how to put up a simple website and to know how to manipulate my own visuals for posting on Facebook or Instagram. I also learned how to edit video and sound for my podcast. This did not take me a long time in the greater scheme of things. Programmers are experts at creating programs and apps that are user friendly. Did it take me some time to do? Sure. But when people say, "time is money," they are not talking about a writer who has not yet monetized. The way I look at it, knowing Photoshop and InDesign and iMovie are all skills that you can capitalize on in case you need a side hustle.

Eek! Did I just say side hustle?

Many authors, the majority of authors, need a side hustle or even a main hustle. If you've gotten to this part in the book and are still fantasizing about being a best-selling author without having any other source of income to back it up with, I have failed in my mission. Yes, it is *possible* to support yourself through writing. But it takes a lot of determination. In general, authors who are willing to add more tools to their arsenals tend to be more resourceful and more learning and effort oriented, and therefore have a better chance at eventually making a living out of writing. In order to stay solvent in the future, you need not to be completely lame at technology. *No one* should boast that they are bad at anything technology related, especially when it is something that a child can do. Being a Luddite is an interesting trait to give one of your characters, but it is not a quality that you want associated with you.

-I don't have any money to spend

Then don't spend any money. Do it yourself. Take advantage of all of the free resources where you can market yourself online to people who are hungry for new content. If you don't have money, however, be realistic in the knowledge that you'll need more time and energy. That's the simple equation. I don't really have any extra money to spend either, so I know that I need to get up an extra hour earlier so that I can do the work that I could've been paying someone else to do.

There are also times when you absolutely *must* make the decision to take money and put it into your writing career, in order to invest in yourself.

-Have you ever bought a pair of shoes for yourself? Of course you have. Because you needed to walk on the street and couldn't do it barefoot.

-Have you ever paid for a haircut or hair color? Of course, you have, because you cannot cut the back of your hair yourself, you don't want to damage your hair or look like a clown, and you need to look decent.

-Have you ever paid for a night out in a restaurant? Yes, because you really wanted to enjoy a relaxing meal with a friend or a loved one.

-Have you ever paid for a massage? Yes, because it makes you feel better, and because you can't do it yourself.

If you realize that the writing services that some people pay for are a *need*, you will understand that paying for them makes sense. I have paid thousands of dollars for editors and for advertising, and I will never consider that to be a waste of money. I have paid for programs to build my mailing list and my website, and that is also money well spent. It's only a waste of money when you drop the ball. Look at it this way, if you invest in yourself, you will see how important these things are for you, you will start to see their value. This is also very motivating. No one wants to waste money. No one likes to throw money at something and then not have it work out. Use the money as motivation. Use the thought or the experience of "wasting" money as an additional pain that can be avoided in the future by simply continuing to push your project forward.

-I don't have the time to write *and* market.

People say this as though it's an "or" thing: as if you are *either* writing, *or* marketing. It is not an "or" thing. Marketing is part of the author's job. It is literally one of the phases of the writing process. It is a nonnegotiable. If you don't have time to do both, cut back on writing and spend some time of each day marketing. If you are spending literally all of your time writing and zero of your time marketing, you are effectively wasting time because your writing will not go as far as it could. So, make the time. If you batch your marketing work, it will not take as much time as you fear. Then again, the more time you put in, or rather the more well focused, well-utilized time you put in, the more success you will have.

-My book is not succeeding because it is too smart and people like dumb stuff

So many people give up on the marketing process early because they see that their book has no traction and no success. Often, they use the craziest excuse to explain why this is: their book is too smart. No, your book is not too smart, and most readers are not dumb. Yes, I know that Fifty Shades of Grey did ridiculously well despite multiple shortcomings but stop using that as an example. I have heard that more than 50 times and I'm even sicker of the excuse that I am of that book. Yes, I admit that book is not my favorite. However, there is something about it that spoke to readers.

Your book is not unsuccessful because it is too smart. Stephen Hawking sold millions of copies of his books, Umberto Eco sold tons of books and had one of his more esoteric books made into a movie. Many of my favorite authors are absolute geniuses, much smarter than you or me. But you know what? People buy and read their books all the time.

If people are not understanding your book, it's not because it's too smart and they are too dumb. Maybe it is because you have not expressed yourself clearly. Maybe your book is not readable. Maybe you describe things in a way that is to obtuse or needlessly complicated. This does not make your book smart; it makes it dumb. If you were smart, you would figure out a way for your message to be understood by your audience. Smart people make complicated concepts easy to digest. Malcolm Gladwell is a great example of this. People love it when they are taught a smart concept or introduced to a cool, complicated world (think Lord of the Rings) in an inclusive way that makes them feel like an insider. Your book is not succeeding because you don't have readers. It is up to you to be honest with yourself and to see why that is.

-I don't want to give any books away because I worked too hard to not make money on them.

Shhhh…Listen! Do you hear that? That's your ego talking!

One of the big pieces of advice when it comes to book marketing is to give away some books for free. This is so incredibly easy to do with eBooks: you are not actually losing any money by doing this, yet so many writers resist doing it because they don't want to give away the fruits of their labor. Giving away the fruits of your labor in order to get readership and reviews is actually part of the labor. It is part of the process. Even best-selling authors do giveaways regularly. If you look at sites like BookBub, you can find any number of bestselling authors on any given day giving away books for free. It's called marketing. You are not better than Stephen King, you are not better than John Grisham and if it's good enough for them it's good enough for you. Giving away books for free paves the way for making money from your books.

-No one supports authors anymore. No one reads books. No one buys books. Publishing is dead.

If I had a penny for every time someone told me that no one supports authors anymore and no one reads books anymore and no one buys books anymore, therefore success is impossible, well, I wouldn't be rich, but I would have a hell of a lot of pennies. It is not up to anyone to support authors. It is up to you as an author to find an audience. It is up to you to give readers what they want, and to make it easy for them to find your book. When you do that, they will read your books and buy your books. There are books out there that sell every day. There are still best sellers, and there are authors who become millionaires. I don't know how this would happen if no one read books anymore. Do you read books? Do you buy books? Do you have favorite authors? Yes, you do. So, you see that what you're saying is patently untrue. Now stop wasting your time with excuses and get marketing.

-I'll start doing the marketing thing when I'm done writing.

So many writers, including me in the past, postpone the marketing thing until they are done writing. They feel that they didn't have time for both writing and marketing, they don't have energy for both, and they don't quite know what they are supposed to be marketing until they are done with it. I can absolutely see how some of those arguments might make their way into your minds. However, a marketing platform is something that takes years to truly gain traction. It takes years to truly build connections with readers and even other writers. It takes years to get comfortable with the marketing techniques that will eventually bring you success. It takes trial and error, and it takes a lot of content for you to become visible online. I don't need to give you the nitty-gritty details of how to market yourself here. Effective ways of marketing yourself pop up all the time. Some stop working and then others start working. There are so many professional marketing gurus out there who do a much better job than I ever will of explaining this, so go look at what they have to say on the subject when you are mentally ready.

What I'm saying here is that chances are that you have a major mindset block when it comes to the marketing, and that's what I'm trying to get out of the way so that you can actually be receptive to the advice of experts. People who are experiencing a mindset block can read every piece of advice there is, and every instruction manual there is, yet never absorb any of it because they are fundamentally blocked against accepting and absorbing that information. I understand that you don't want to market your specific book too early in the game. There are 1000 things that can happen to that book. You can change the title, you can change the cover, you can change your main character, and understandably, you don't want to be promoting any of these specifics. But you do want to be promoting yourself as an author. This is something that you need to be doing all the time. This way, when a new book comes out, you'll have less of a mountain to climb.

-The "build it and they will come" excuse

This excuse is one of the ones that drives me the craziest. Contained in this excuse is the implicit belief that if you write something good, you don't need to market yourself. Built into this is the justification that if you are not getting immediate attention for your book, it's because it's fundamentally not that good, therefore not worth marketing. This circular argument makes absolutely no sense. Suffice it to say that this mindset is not true, and it's very harmful. There is a lot of noise out there and you need to break through it to get any attention, no matter how good your book is.

-There is too much noise out there

Speaking of noise, this is the final excuse I'll be covering. So many authors say that there's too much noise out there for them to get attention, get traction, and make a difference. They bring up the figures they have researched about how much new content comes out every day, how many books are published each year, how many YouTube videos are uploaded each minute, how many Instagram posts come up each nanosecond, and whatever other stupid figure they want to use to justify not marketing themselves.

The time they took to research this useless information would have been much better spent marketing themselves. No matter how much noise there is out there, if you position yourself correctly, you can be found, either online or in the real world. It doesn't take an SEO genius to figure this out, either. In just a few days, I was able to make myself infinitely more searchable and findable online, and I've helped the writers in my writing group do this as well.

Here's some super quick and effective advice to start that will start to move the needle:

-Choose a form of your name that is unique.

-Choose a unique hashtag that describes your style for use by your fans.

-Appear at events that gather your specific micro niche. Niche down. Find very specific readers and appeal to them.

But you know this. Or if you didn't know this, it's incredibly easy to figure out. It's applying this knowledge that is scary and time-consuming, isn't it?

Chapter 5: TYPICAL Writer's Block ADVICE

(Whether it works, and why it just defers the pain)

I mentioned in the introduction that most books on writer's block suggest physical exercise, or breathing, or meditation exercises you can do to supposedly alleviate writer's block. When I was doing the research for this book, the same advice kept coming up over and over, in books and articles spanning decades. If this advice was a perfect solution, everyone would adopt it and people wouldn't need to keep doling it out. I will briefly go over each of these pieces of advice here, along with my thoughts on the degree to which they do or don't work, because some of these suggestions can be good general ideas to have in your back pocket to reinforce the mindset we are working on, while others are a waste of time.

The simple point is, you can do all the writing exercises and meditation in the world, but it won't help you to write, let alone publish and promote a book if your same old mindset persists. That writer's block will just keep coming back, sneaking back in, and making you suffer. These pieces of advice may be alleviating some symptoms, but they do nothing to address the root cause of your lack of success.

This is how the writer's block fallacy augments its pernicious effects: writers keep looking for ways to solve a small part of the problem, and the solutions steer them away from addressing what is actually happening.

Let's talk about the typical advice for writer's block.

Go for a walk

It was a gorgeous day for a hike. I could always count on the scenery around the trail just off of Mandeville Canyon, a wilderness right in the center of Los Angeles, to inspire me. At least, that was my justification for joining a friend for a walk, when I knew that I really needed to get some writing done. This particular piece of writing wasn't for one of my multiple novels-in-progress: it was an article for the magazine at which I worked and suffice it to say that I did not find the assignment very inspiring.

I reasoned with myself that my walking buddy might be a good sounding board for my various ideas on how to make a boring subject a little more exciting. But my friend wanted to talk about something else entirely, and frankly, who could blame her? After an hour on the trail, I realized that I wasn't enjoying myself at all, knowing that since my article was due the next day, I would now have to work late into the night. Even worse, I knew that by not prioritizing my writing when it was crucial, I was probably going to be turning in something sub-par, something I would not be particularly proud to see my byline under. Also, I realized that I was so busy agonizing over how irresponsible I was being that I wasn't even listening to my friend at all. I was being a bad friend on top of being a bad writer.

I think it's a great idea to go for a walk. But it's a great idea in general, not a stand-alone strategy for eliminating writer's block. Going outside is "scientifically proven" (depending on which research you believe) to improve your mood and aid in creative thinking and problem-solving but it won't get to the root of your writer's block.

-Wendy Suzuki, author of "Healthy Brain, Happy Life," states that exercise improves productivity, focus, memory, and problem-solving, all of which are building blocks of creativity.

-A study by Stanford researchers Marily Oppezzo and Daniel Schwartz showed that creative thinking improves during walking and shortly thereafter. This study, however, argues that walking does not help with focus.

-Several recent studies have demonstrated that being in nature improves cognitive abilities, however for the full effect, you would need to be in nature and "unplugged" for **four days** or more, according to Ruth Ann Atchley from the University of Kansas.

The conclusion of these studies supports my basic theory that, while exercise is great, don't fall into the trap of believing that it is a magic bullet for writer's block. You'll end up a very fit, but frustrated writer! That time you spend going outside should be something that you do for the enjoyment of it. If you're doing it with the goal of hopefully writing more, don't you agree that just staying home and writing would technically be a more direct path to that result than hitting a hiking trail?

Life is all about balance. Personally, going outside is an important aspect of my life, but it's completely independent from the time I devote to writing. For sure, there are worse things than going outside, and especially being active outside. Many writers I interviewed mentioned that a morning run or walk is part of their writing routine. There's the magic word: *routine*. They're not viewing it as a fix. Making a walk part of your routine promotes health and a balanced life. Don't try to make it into a solution for writer's block- you'll suck the joy out of it.

Eliminate distractions

My husband announced he was going on yet another business trip. His business trips are almost never to exciting spots, so he was shocked when I begged to join him. Not to knock Charlotte, NC, but I'm not a NASCAR fan and it was the middle of winter, so he reminded me that there would be literally nothing to do there. "Perfect," I told him. "I'm going to eliminate distractions and get so much writing done." Without the usual housework, without friends to distract me or the dog to take for walks, without my volunteer or work obligations, this stay in Charlotte was going to be the most productive time in my life. We checked into the nondescript hotel suite, I queued up the local food delivery services, got out my laptop, and...

Well, I didn't leave the hotel room for five days...scary, I know. I felt like I was doing *something* but honestly, I don't think I got that much writing done. For some reason, the whole zero distractions, zero obligations thing did not work out for me. Also, would I be able to recreate this distraction-free zone at home? Doubtful. Would I want to? Probably not.

I don't know that distractions are actually a huge part of the writer's block equation. I have ADHD- mild according to me, severe according to others close to me. Do I get distracted? Always. Like probably every 30 seconds to 5 minutes. Do I still finish books? Yes.

Now, let's take a look at this radical distraction-elimination as a solution to ban writer's block. First of all, it implies lots of solitude. Solitude can be scary. Writing in a vacuum can be even more difficult. Some writers will lock themselves in a simple, cell-like room with no phone or internet, or pay money for an app that eliminates all distractions from their computer screen, or even buy an old-fashioned typewriter-like device to that effect... Oooh! Sounds great! Just you, your thoughts...and your writer's block! Seriously, this radical isolation approach can leave you too exposed to your obsessing about your writer's block, especially if you haven't gotten down to changing your mindset about it.

I know one writer- I'll call her Jen to protect her identity- who saved up her hard-earned money to rent an apartment in a tiny town in Scotland for a week, so she could finally get her long-simmering book ideas down on paper, or at least down on her laptop. She convinced her supportive but skeptical husband to take a week off of work to babysit the kids. After a long and complicated journey, Jen realized that she would actually only be in Scotland for four days (she lives in LA). The pressure was on to start writing...but the pictures hadn't been able to do justice to just how freezing it would be in the charming apartment she'd rented, which made it a lot less conducive to work than her local cafe or home office, and instead of finding her muse, she spent half her time on the phone crying to her husband and friends about how much she missed her kids, and the other half at the pub down the street. She returned from Scotland disappointed in herself, a few thousand dollars poorer, and with no work to show for it all. She had learned the hard way that the act of getting away from it all is not a fix-all for writer's block. Not to mention, she could have been writing during all those hours spent planning her trip and in transit and could have put that money towards renting a co-working space aimed at creatives or going on a well-organized group retreat with supportive writers and knowledgeable coaches.

The good news is that this trip was a wake-up call for Jen. After just a couple one-on-one coaching sessions to help her to put the Spalmorum Method into practice, her first finished book is being shopped around to agents.

Once you have transformed your mindset, eliminating distractions is something that you will naturally actively seek out, and at that point you will be able to determine which distractions are most harmful to your own productivity, and which "background noise" is actually helpful in some way.

I usually do the very thing most of these articles say is a huge "no-no": I like to have a Google search window open in case I need to look up a concept or an idea on the fly. The less barriers I have to doing that quick piece of research, the faster I can get back to writing, all the while staying in the groove. Of course, that doesn't mean you should be having a web-surfing free-for-all when you're meant to be writing. But knowing that I can do a targeted search when needed really helps me. Also, I am as social media and device obsessed as the next person (actually, probably even more so- my screen time figures make me shudder) so I know first-hand that disabling messaging apps to give yourself distraction-free writing sprints may be a good plan in general... however, it won't help in the least if you are still suffering from writer's block.

I also like working in a quiet public space so I can feel "connected to the world" yet not distracted. I am not a hermit at heart, though, so if you are, maybe you like the idea of a cabin in the woods (I recommend finding one that is relatively local to you so you don't waste time on travel like Jen did), and in that case, I say go for it- but fix your mindset first.

Play

Many people who have penned guides for getting though writer's block will recommend taking a lighter approach to the problem: creative play, they say, where there is no expectation of a real product that will be judged in any way, can be a solution for getting the creative juices flowing again. This is true to a certain degree: if the goal is to just *generally* get back into a creative groove, this technique can work wonders. However, play will not do anything for you when it comes to finishing, editing, or promoting your book.

This is not to say that play and having fun are bad. Fun is always a worthwhile pursuit. But for most writers, writing *is* fun. Until it's not.

If you simply adopt our mindset hacks through the Spalmorum Method, you'll remove most of the perceived pain from the "painful" parts of the process, and each aspect of writing can become something that is fun and creatively rewarding. Even the "hard" part, the part that is harder to spin into a "fun" mindset: editing and selling your book, can be made fun:

-Interacting with all kinds of people.

-Learning new skills.

-Seeing your marketing strategy as a puzzle.

Play that is designed as a distraction from the task of getting your book done and out there is not really helpful in and of itself. Making the components of the writing process more streamlined, and therefore more fun, however, can definitely work.

A little note on pursuits/distractions such as reading, painting, playing or listening to music, and enjoying movies or TV shows: don't beat yourself up if you're doing them. We all seek out balance, and even though cutting these activities down significantly is often necessary for success, it's a really hard process for a lot of people. If/when you do seek out distractions, don't do these activities mindlessly. Do them consciously, mindfully, with the goal of using them to feed and complement your writing practice. You may have less time for leisure and other fun activities, so really make them count.

A few ideas:

-Adopt a new creative or athletic activity that a character in your book participates in.

-Paint something that reflects a setting in your novel, or that could influence the cover art.

-Watch a movie or read a book and observe how each scene moves the plot forward. Observe stylistic elements that are more or less successful, or how the dialogue works.

-Listen to music to learn about pacing, rhythm, style, and delivery. Also, lyrics can influence title or plot.

-Hang out with writers and other creative entrepreneurs who can motivate you as you socialize. Speaking of this, a common piece of advice is:

Reach out to a friend

This can be a good technique, however if you have not hacked your mindset already, it can backfire.

So many times, we reach out to our friends when we have a problem or issue, and they try to "solve" it by giving us "solutions" that may actually not help at all. Many of us reach out to too many friends and get several pieces of crazy-making contradictory advice. There's also the "misery loves company" mindset where you all spend your time focusing on the negative, and hence feeling the pain of not finishing and publishing your book all the more intensely.

Here are some of the types of friends that writers may encounter while desperately searching for someone, anyone, to talk them off the writer's block ledge:

-The friend who tries to assuage the pain of writing block by coming up with the "ultimate solution": stop writing! After all, isn't that the thing that's causing you pain?

-The friend who tries to "help" by talking about some other friend of theirs who had "no problem" writing and has happily published with no issues, and with great success. How inspiring!

-The friend who offers to help keep you on track... with advice and feedback while they're at it. This friend is almost never a writer themselves. And usually, this friend is just a little bit sadistic.

-The friend who has never written a thing but who keeps reminding you oh-so-helpfully that "writers write" or "if you're waiting instead of writing, you're a waiter, not a writer." These are platitudes and frankly, I've met some happy and dedicated waiters who are also excellent writers. In fact, in terms of character inspiration, it's a pretty great job to have!

-The friend who just read this one totally inspiring article about writing and is now certified to tell you that everything you've been doing is completely wrong.

A crucial recommendation would be to only reach out to friends who understand what you're going through, who are going through it, or have been through it. Also, in general, and especially as a writer, choose your close friends wisely. You don't want any sanctimonious, jealous, or negative people around you. Set up the expectation for any communication about writing or creativity early on. You can say things like "let's pledge to be positive for the whole conversation," or "I just need someone to listen, not necessarily to fix this," or "let's reaffirm each other's qualities as writers and creatives." This may sound cheesy-all right, you can remove the "may" from that statement, but believe me, it works a lot better than the alternative.

Commiserating may seem fun, but it literally contains the root for the word "misery." Don't get stuck in that trap. Misery loves company, and miserable company feeds, perpetuates, and reinforces misery, and hence pain.

The better person to reach out to would be a *mentor*: someone who has encountered the sort of success you seek, and who is generous enough to share their advice and the good, the bad, and the ugly. Giving success a human face helps you to see that it's possible and to understand what it takes to attain what you want.

Create a routine

If you're reading this book, your routine is clearly not working for you, or at least some part of it is not working. If you try to create a routine before you've fixed the root of your writer's block problem, you are just going to be reaffirming your bad habits. Also, routine is OK for the writing part, but after that, ensuring your success will require breaking out of your routine and going above and beyond anything you have ever done before this point. If you are too comfortable in your routine, stepping out of it will be painful. This will signal to your brain that the new activity is bad. This is not the correct conclusion of you want to progress. A routine is not enough to make the quantum leap from aspiring writer to successful author.

And yes, creating a positive and productive routine could be helpful during the writing stage. Most importantly, it may help you to form good habits, and help prevent the formation of bad writing habits. The power of habit is enormous, as you may have observed in your own life.

Susan Courtney, of Johns Hopkins University, explains that this has to do with the prefrontal cortex, the part of your brain that needs to be activated to change a habit. The problem is that the prefrontal cortex is "easily distracted and doesn't work well when you're stressed or tired. When that part of the brain is vulnerable, those habits that are hardwired into other parts of the brain automatically take over." "Stressed or tired" totally describes your brain on writer's block. It's part of the pain of writer's block, isn't it?

What kind of bad writing habits do I mean? Here are just a few- do any of them sound like something you've done before? For me, it would be more like *all of them*.

-Rewarding yourself for writing a small unit of text with something unhealthy- cookies, gallons of coffee, a cigarette or two... or something that takes too much time or energy away from writing, such as watching an episode or three of your favorite TV show, taking a trip to the craft store and then starting on a whole new DIY project...

-Procrastinating, but then justifying it to yourself by calling your procrastinating activities "self-care." Finishing a long-term and deeply meaningful project like your book is more impactful to your mental and spiritual well-being than all the face masks and bubble baths or meditation in the world.

-Spending more creative energy on your excuses than on actually producing any work. Well, at least you know you've still got a working imagination, I guess.

-Calling your other writer friend who is also suffering from writer's block and venting about the same old issue. And not even recording the conversation to use as an example of "boring dialogues my characters should *not* be having."

-Consistently "operating" on not enough sleep but being proud of it because you think it makes you a tortured artist. Even if you were on a literal deadline from an actual professional authority figure in your industry, sleep is a crucial ingredient for creativity.

-Obsessively self-editing before you're done. Don't do it. It's really hard to preserve a positive mindset when you're judging yourself every step of the way. Every author, even the most successful one, writes flaming crap at some point. And eventually, it gets edited out. Just keep moving forward first.

While writer's block is still causing you so much pain, you will find it really hard to develop a healthy writing and promotion routine.

Once you've broken through the limiting mindsets you were fostering, however, you will start to form *good* writing habits, and be able to have a more productive attitude towards the kind of routine you may want to establish.

Use writing prompts

Aren't writing prompts fun? I like to use prompts in my writing group when one or more of my writers is struggling because they're taking their story too seriously and feel like they've sucked the joy out of it.

But here is one major caveat: rather than use general, "wild card" writing prompts like the ones you'll find all over Instagram or Pinterest (you know the ones- I just did a google search for "writing prompts" and came across a trove of silliness... totally fine if you're 12 years old and looking to produce a few paragraphs on Wattpad, but not if you're serious about your novel or memoir), I like to use *contextual prompts* that can be used in the novel in progress, if not in their exact form, at least as inspiration for plot, setting, or character.

But seriously: if all it takes to shift your writer's block is a fun writing exercise, you don't really have writer's block. Prompts may work to flesh out a character or introduce a plot twist but remember that brief lapses in inspiration are totally normal and are not the same thing as writer's block.

So if you're constantly using general "just for fun" writing prompts to kick-start your creativity, and it starts to happen during most of your writing sessions, you're not just playing around, you're actually rewarding a

procrastination habit- because these prompts can be fun-
they're the writing equivalent of having a donut or two to
motivate yourself to work out- and the results over time
can be just as disastrous.

Just Write

One of my "not favorite" pieces of writing advice is
"writers write," or "just write." *Dude.* "Just writing" will
not take you from aspiring writer to successful author.
There is so much more to it than that.

- "Just writing" will give you words and maybe some
stories, but it is not enough to yield a high-quality
published book you can be proud of.

- "Just writing" may pressure you into producing
quantity but not quality.

- "Just writing" may give you a monumental work of
rambling, barely editable drivel that will only ever make a
good doorstop, if you decide to waste the paper and print
it out.

It's never "just" about writing.

-It's about telling a good story in a way that is clear,
entertaining, touching, and gives your readers characters
they will root for and against, and unforgettable settings
they can see in their mind's eye.

-It's about having the self-awareness to detect your
shortcomings as a writer, while being kind and patient
enough with yourself to correct them.

-It's about having the humility required to take the constructive advice of editors and reviewers and use it to improve your book.

-It's about having the steadfastness to see your whole book through to completion, and then to have the courage to promote it, without giving up.

-It's about being realistic enough to realize that books don't sell themselves, and that usually, no one cares about your work as much as you do, yet to be optimistic enough to see that sometimes, a work will speak to people, and will encounter an exponential rate of success.

Here is my conclusion, when it comes to all of these "helpful" "Fixes" for writer's block:

The difference between an aspiring writer and a successful author does not come down to little "tricks" or "hacks" that temporarily alleviate the pain of writer's block or help you get more words on the page.

Those are a band-aid. Healing the cause of the pain comes down to mindset, which will yield the actual things that will make you perform the actions that will get your book written, edited, published, and sold.

As a bonus, here are some off-the-cuff rebuttals of the various pieces of advice I've collected, both on social media and in the early days of my writing group. You've probably heard these too at some point. I think that these betray the pain that writer's block and not achieving writing dreams is causing these writers, and frankly, I've been there before, too. With most of these responses, it sometimes felt like I was listening to a previous *me*.

Write every day.

"I mean, that's the ideal, right? And usually, almost always, I do that. But sometimes, it's going to be less than a paragraph of absolute crap. Does that count?" -Joe B.

"Basically, with this advice, I feel like if I miss a day I I'm a total failure as a writer and, by extension, as a human being." -Carrie P.

"How is pushing through and writing each day possible? Why can't you understand that my writer's block is paralyzing?" -Patricia G.

Wake up an hour earlier.

"You tryin' to kill me?" -Barbara M.

"I can't even speak when I'm tired, let alone write." -Xavier E.

"What if I finally start to write and then have to interrupt myself because now I'm late to work, and I haven't showered and have to wear the same thing as yesterday and everyone thinks I'm doing a walk of shame except it is way more shameful than that? I can't get really into doing something if I know that I'm going to need to be somewhere soon!" -Jen C.

Get out of the house.

"My kids won't let me!" -Mandy F.

"People-watching in the places I'm supposed to be writing in is my favorite distraction. Living in LA, every single person in the coffee shops I've visited while trying to escape is also a writer, so instead of writing, I'm analyzing each one of them, wondering about their level of success, what they're working on, why they're so good at typing, that sort of thing. Last time, I literally was sidetracked by this girl's shoes (Golden Goose, $1000 or something for a pair of sneakers that comes lovingly pre-trashed…. I Googled them on the spot) and started wondering if she'd paid for them with some mega book advance the likes of which I'll never see. Didn't get any writing done." -Angel K.

Unplug.

"Some of us (me) are too neurotic for this and the anxiety over unplugging may be distracting. It might work great if you let it. But I wouldn't know. What if I need to get in touch with someone? What if there's an emergency? What if someone is making a fun plan and I can get out of here and do something else?" -Jordan G.

NEVER skip writing.

"Sometimes life throws other priorities or challenges your way." -Micah C.

"Don't add guilt to my plate, *thankyouverymuch*." -Chloe F.

"There is nothing like a stern edict to make me rebel. Just ask every single gym I've signed up for and the co-working spaces I don't frequent ever again once I've paid for the month up front." -Jill R.

Chapter 6: About Mindset

In reading this book, in truly absorbing its message, and in doing the transformative work, you're taking crucial steps towards your success as an author today: you're willing to acknowledge the pain that writer's block is causing you, and you're willing to face some tough realities and to transform your mindset in a way that will alleviate most, if not all, of your issues with the *real* writer's block.

Transforming my mindset was a tough transition for me to make, and I didn't have a crystal-clear blueprint for it at the time. All I knew was that the way I was doing it wasn't working for me. I couldn't stand being this way for much longer. You must understand that is *so* much harder, emotionally, to be unsuccessful than to be successful. Once I figured out the importance of mindset, and of adopting growth mindsets while ditching limiting, fixed mindsets, I understood why such a great majority of otherwise excellent writers have few chances of finishing a book, of finding an agent, or of getting published or even of self-publishing. Those who commit to a healthier mindset, however, not only feel better in general, but have an exponentially better chance of achieving those goals.

Transforming your mindset not only instantly gets rid of the pain caused by writer's blocks of all kinds, it truly is the main element that sets you up for success.

To be a successful author, you need to stop thinking like an "aspiring writer" and start acting like

a kick-ass creative entrepreneur. This implies
ACTION.

We're going to be talking about action soon, because it is one of the magical ingredients for success as an author. It also happens to be the thing that definitely does not happen when one is dealing with any of the varieties of writer's block. When action is blocked by negative mindsets, progress seems impossible. The pain caused by your writer's block has weakened you. It has made you feel that you are not able to live any other way. The pain becomes your reality, and what you're comfortable with. This is a result of the real writer's block: a wall comprised of mindset after negative mindset. These mindset "blocks" are strong. As humans, once we adopt a belief, we are very slow to let it go. Some of these negative mindsets are masquerading as confidence, or self-worth, or protection. But the reality is far from that. Let me explain. First, let's talk about what mindset is, and why it's so powerful.

What is Mindset?

Figuring out how to hack your mindset includes elements from both neuroscience and psychology. Basically, you have to understand what's going on in your brain, observe it, accept it, figure out the causes, and then train your brain to act differently. We are not going to get into technical brain research or talk about changing links between synapses or neurons. We don't need an MRI to see that the pain of writer's block comes from within. You did this to yourself with your negative mindsets. But don't worry, you are not going to need to get out of it alone!

Mindset is an over-arching term for the collection of beliefs, attitudes, and thoughts each of us has. Mindset affects or is affected by predispositions, inclinations, and habits. Each of us has developed a specific mindset shaped by our biology, our family, our environment, and our society. Mindset largely dictates how we react to situations, how we approach a problem, and even affects our chances of success in any given endeavor. Your mindset, or the set of beliefs that you hold true, can determine what you want, why you want it, and whether you are ever able to attain it.

Mindset has long been the focus for Carol Dweck, an education professor at Stanford University. In fact, she is probably the reason we even speak of mindset. Dr Dweck was the first to lay out the differences between a *fixed* mindset and a *growth* mindset. Dweck's conclusions, in a nutshell: people with a fixed mindset focus on performance. They believe that people are born with a preset level of talent and ability and other characteristics that are fixed and unchangeable. If you believe that your personality, intelligence, and talent have been pre-ordained by some higher power, you will not be as likely to do what is necessary to increase them.

If you have a fixed mindset:

-You are more likely to automatically begin to avoid challenges and situations where the outcome is not certain.

-You are likely to avoid situations where you may be made to look less cool, or less intelligent.

- You will probably do everything possible to avoid rejection or judgment. Anything that makes you feel like a loser will be viewed as highly undesirable. As such, you will be shrinking your world to only things that are not a challenge. I am guessing that is the opposite sentiment of what originally made you want to write.

Those with a growth mindset believe that they can, well, grow. This means a focus on improvement over time, and on the process, and leaning into the challenge.

If you have a growth mindset:

-You strongly believe that you can develop and strengthen abilities and talents by devoting time, effort, and energy to them.

-Challenges feel rewarding- *whether they are conquered completely or not.*

-You feel that each opportunity for growth and progress is positive.

-You learn to seek out learning experiences.

-Failure and disappointment do not exist. They are simply opportunities for progress.

The very same situation can be viewed through the lens either mindset.

Here is the basic premise: Anna is 46. She's always wanted to write but was busy with raising her two kids and with working from home as a marketer. Now, with the kids out of the house, and having managed to scale back her earning requirements through downsizing, she's in a position to try. She sits down and tries to write a book, but the ideas that had excited her before she got started now feel silly and basic. Her characters are boring. She's re-read the little she has written and finds her sentence structure and choice of words elementary. Now, she is stuck.

Mindset A:

My book is so boring. Everyone else has had these ideas before and has written about them better. I don't have the skills or the talent to write a novel anyway. I should have gone to school for this, but now I don't have time to anymore. This is silly- I am too old to think of becoming a novelist now!

Mindset B:

My ideas were exciting to me once, so where can I find that excitement again? Perhaps I need to think creatively about my characters. I'm not loving my limited vocabulary, so I'm going to start looking up some lists of creative words I can use for some of my passages. However, some readers may appreciate simplicity. I'll find an editor later to help me to whip this into shape once I'm finished. Good thing I now have time to dedicate to my writing, I'm lucky that I had my career first, with all the learning that goes with it, and now I can pour that into my writing. It's hard now, but if I go step by step, I'll get there.

As someone who strongly believes in a growth mindset and who has learned to embrace this mindset as often as I can (it's not about perfection, people!), I know that mindset is not something one is born with. It is something that we are trained to embrace, either through some personal conviction molded from experiences and reflection, or by a mentor or mentors who made us see the light. Children who were treated in such a way that they ended up feeling concerned about judgment, who attached love to success and performance, and who grew fearful of not being as good as their peers, are more likely to develop a fixed mindset, and more likely to get mired in the bog of negative ideas that having a fixed mindset can allow in. The opposite case can also, oddly enough, contribute to a fixed mindset. Parents who constantly tell children that they are smart, beautiful, or talented can, instead of creating confidence, create fear that, if their smarts, beauty, or talent suddenly are challenged by someone or something, their value as a person decreases irremediably. Basically, your problem mindset is *not* proof that you had terrible parenting, so don't call your parents and blame them!

Also, having grown up to develop a fixed mindset is not a death sentence. You can definitely work your way out of it. Some people were taught to explore, and enjoy challenges, and grew up understanding that mistakes were merely stumbling blocks, not roadblocks, and that they allowed for learning and growth. These people may be ahead of the game when it comes to mindset, but that doesn't mean that they don't need to keep training their brain to stay within this growth mindset. In fact, when you have a growth mindset, you will see that there is always room for growth and improvement. You develop a craving for growth and improvement. There is no limit.

If you fear that you have a fixed mindset:

-Focus on the process.

-Focus on hard work.

-Select tasks that offer more opportunities for growth.

-Develop a routine that encourages consistency.

-Pride yourself on kindness, collaboration, and communication above all things.

-Treat yourself kindly.

-Stop expecting immediate results.

So why is mindset so important? Mindset completely informs the way in which we react to a situation. We can see the same exact situation, and then deal with it, react to it, and interpret it a completely different way. Two people can have writers block, but one person can view it as something that can and should be changed. They will note the pain it causes and use it as impetus to change, whereas the other writer can become distraught and feel victimized by the situation. That writer will tend to focus on the pain and use it to justify quitting.

Need a real-life example of this idea in action? Here it is: Nicki reached out via Facebook Messages a while back. She's a young writer who took writing classes at her university and did well. Thanks to one of her professors, who encouraged her, not one, but two of her pieces of short fiction had been published in anthologies. Now out of school and navigating "real life," she was hoping to parlay her education into writing a full-length novel.

The problem was, now that she no longer had the constant reassurance and support of her university professors, she felt alone in the world. She was having trouble moving past the initial concept, and now was growing desperate that she didn't actually have all the skills and knowledge she needed to write a full-length book. Now that she was out of college, she admitted, she felt that she had no way of making up the knowledge she thought she needed. "I mean, I know how to write a short story," she lamented, "but I was never taught to write a full-length novel. And I don't have the time or money to go back to school!"

Nikki displayed all of the signs of information block. Also, her writer's block was so painful to her, and her mindset was so incredibly fixed, that she literally could not see the truth. Her well-meaning professor, with her praise, had made Nikki dependent on that support and feedback. Nikki had performed well, she now craved the praise, but she believed that her professor and the structure of school were some of the non-negotiable elements of her success to that point. Without them, she was stuck.

I had to gently guide Nikki into seeing that her time at the university had taught her to learn and think and research, and to apply those skills to the real world. Her capacity for learning and improving was not finite, and her professor's praise and aid were just signs that she was very capable and had a promising career ahead of her. These were just small successes in a long string of future successes. Nikki finally came to see her block as a symptom of the high standards she had developed while at school. She looked at her situation objectively and saw that the intense pain her perceived knowledge block was causing her was actually a good sign- a sign that she realized that there was something lacking in her know-how. Once she figured out which pieces of knowledge she was missing, she would go about acquiring them.

"Why don't you reach out to your professor and see how she's doing? Share your experiences with writing long form with her," I suggested. Nikki was floored. She admitted that she had been subconsciously seeing the chapter of college as forever closed. This was yet another symptom of her fixed mindset. She is now happy to call her professor, a novelist in her own right, a mentor. Nikki will no doubt suffer other episodes of writer's block, but with practice, she will learn to power through. Having a "crisis," where the pain of writer's block became strong enough to reach out to a virtual stranger, is the breakthrough that finally got Nikki to see her fixed mindset for what it was.

How can you tell what kind of mindset you have?

If you're honest with yourself and look back at how you have dealt with obstacles and challenges in your past, a pattern will begin to emerge.

-What do you do when faced with a difficult problem? Do you work on it step-by-step, believing that at some point you will probably eventually be able to solve it, or at the very least view it as a challenge and a useful growth experience? Or do you get frustrated at the apparent impossibility of solving it, and then get depressed and conclude that your intelligence and talents were not up to snuff? Almost more importantly, when you failed at something that you assume that you failed at because it was too challenging for you, did you then dread the judgments and scrutiny of others?

-Do you believe that certain people were born more intelligent and talented than others, and that they are automatically at an advantage for the rest of their lives because of this?

-Do you believe that there's not much you can do to modify or improve your abilities and personality, or do you think that these can be constantly improved upon?

-Do you believe that people can change?

-Do you believe that learning decreases after a certain age, or that your brain's ability to absorb new materials and skills goes downhill at a certain age?

-Do you believe that some people are simply not talented at a certain thing, and that no amount of work can bring them up to someone else's level in artistic, physical, or intellectual pursuits? Or do you believe that practice, hard work, and persistence are more valuable?

Which way of thinking seems to you like it would lead to more success? Would you rather think that you haven't succeeded because you are lacking the fundamental talent to succeed, or that you simply haven't succeeded…yet?

Intellectually, I am sure that you can see how a growth mindset is of course preferable. You may even have given the "correct" answers to the questions above- but be honest: sometimes, even though you know how you *should* be approaching a situation, you can't quite get to a place where you have *truly* adopted that mindset.

Also, breaking mindset into fixed and growth mindset is a little too simplistic.

At Spalmorum, we have observed that mindset can come under many guises. There are many little micro-mindsets, which we pick up along the way, over a lifetime, and these in turn shape our beliefs and behaviors. Our mindsets limit us in so many ways, and it is important to acknowledge how difficult it is to abandon a mindset once adopted.

Steps you can take to change a harmful mindset:

1)   **Feel and identify the pain of your specific "writer's block."**
2)   **Be honest with yourself and figure out which mindset is causing this block.**
3)   **Do the work to ditch the mindset.**

4)   Adopt a new, helpful, healthier mindset to fill the blank space.

Easier said than done, right? Don't worry, we are going to break this all down. We're not going to deal with every single one of the mindsets that we hold, because they are legion! There are so very many of our beliefs that can lead to self-defeating behavior, or behavior that is not optimal, but we are going to focus on the major mindsets that hold us back from writing and creative production in general.

HARMFUL MINDSETS
(That many writers exhibit)

-Victim Mentality

We mentioned this briefly in the ego chapter, but we'll dive in a little deeper here, with examples. With this mindset, others are responsible for your success or lack thereof. Agents and publishers are the enemy, Amazon is evil, that troll who gave you a bad review is responsible for your failure, and there is nothing you can do about it. Life is a struggle, and there are numerous blocks in your way, none of which you have any power to do anything about. Nothing will ever change, because for some reason you were born unlucky. There is an invisible sign on your forehead that tells others to mistreat you. Better just to give up.

One of the writers I've been trying to help along the way (I'll call her Patricia) was displaying a classic case of victim mentality. Patricia also happens to be a chef, and she had dreamed of publishing something that was a hybrid between a memoir and a recipe book. But the excuses kept on coming as to why this could not be done:

- "I'm Hispanic, and I'm a woman," she said. "Those are two strikes against me."

- "Have you ever heard of Laura Esquivel?" I asked. "She wrote this little thing called *Like Water for Chocolate*. It's like a novel with recipes. It did fairly well. They made a little movie from it, too. It was nominated for a Golden Globe. No big deal."

There are a ton of other female writers out there that are hugely successful. Some are from India, or from Africa, or from truly repressive societies. But Patricia was already looking for more reasons why she was a victim.

"I've had a really difficult life," she said.

"That's a bummer, but you're doing great now," I countered. "You can pour that into your memoir. Easy lives rarely make for good stories."

"I'm all alone, with no support, no connections" she said.

"What am I, chopped liver?"

I didn't even bother to bring up the other people in our close-knit writing group who have always been beyond encouraging, or Patricia's ultra-devoted spouse, because these excuses are not real. They are all in her head. This is probably the right moment to mention that Patricia is not just a chef, she is a chef for one of the most famous bands in the world, as well as for a famous author who happens to be Hispanic and a woman. Talk about connections!

"Well, I gave my boss something I had written to read, and she told me I needed to work on it more and finish my book before she would even show it to her agent. So, there's no chance."

Wow. Patricia had access to someone who was willing to show her work to her high-powered agent. She had given her good feedback, which was to polish it and finish it, and because Patricia wasn't willing to put in the work, she was going to blame everyone and everything but herself?

Classic victim mentality.

In Patricia's case, I must admit that her victim mentality is so deep-seated that we are having a hard time dislodging it. She is resisting change because the pain of her victim mentality is the pain she is familiar with. In her mind, the pain she knows is preferable to the potential pain of the unknown. I know this book is supposed to be positive, but I can't get any further with Patricia for now because Patricia has learned how to numb herself to that particular pain. She is currently unable to see the path to success because she is unwilling. But Patricia is still young. Hopefully she will come to her senses before it's too late.

-Inferiority/ Impostor Syndrome

You are forever an aspiring writer, because you're not good/creative/dedicated enough to be a "real" author. Therefore, since you are not worthy of being a "real" author, you should not put in the work or seize opportunities that come your way. Any success makes you uncomfortable, because now, with more attention and exposure, someone will discover that you are a big fake. You'll never promote yourself because you are positive that people will point out that you are just not as good as other authors. In your mind, you don't have the education, the experience, or the talent, and you probably never will.

There was a writer in my group, Rachel, who stopped coming to our meetings. This was a real pity, because her writing was full of promise, and her story had a lot of potential. Some people stop coming to writing group because "life happens": a new job, childcare responsibilities, travel, or taking care of an aging parent. These excuses are all totally valid. Dealing with these all-too-common human situations only enriches your experience and your writing, if you let it. However, some people drop out of writing group because of problematic mindsets, and when I see that they are on the cusp of a possible mindset breakthrough, I'll call them on it. In this case, I literally picked up the phone and called Rachel.

"I don't come to group anymore because I'm wasting everyone else's time," said Rachel.

"Wasting their time? Why?"

"Well…they're real writers."

"And you're not?" I asked.

"I mean…" sputtered Rachel. She was in the throes of imposter syndrome but coming out and admitting that she didn't consider herself to be a real writer was super painful. Good.

"When did you realize that you weren't a real writer? When did you figure out that you actually were never going to finish your book?" I asked.

"I mean, I want to finish my book. I'm working on it when I can. I just don't always have new work to go over and I don't want the others to get impatient with me."

She was getting defensive, which was a good thing, as long as it was paired with clarity and self-honesty.

"So, you *are* a real writer. And don't worry, the only person who is impatient with you is you. The other writers move forward or not regardless of how you're doing. Your progress doesn't really impact them that much. Sure, I might be happier to see you making more progress, but really, it's on you. I consider you like I consider all my other writers."

I'm happy to report that Rachel is starting to consider herself as a "real" writer. An imperfect one, one who sometimes fails to make the progress she was hoping to. One who often has trouble translating her grandiose visions into the right words. But a writer, nonetheless.

There is no such thing as a "more real writer." Yes, there are better writers and worse writers, but there is movement within those categories, and those categories are not always tied to success.

-Entitled Mindset

With this mindset, you secretly believe that you are "owed" certain things due to your degrees, your memberships, your hard work, your status, or your intellectual or personal qualities. Maybe everyone has always told you that you are super creative. Now, you believe that this means you're your book has a better chance of being a bestseller. You almost think people should feel lucky to read or to be given the chance to review such creative work. Or maybe you attended a well-regarded writing program or writing class. Now that you've done the time and earned the grade, you feel "accredited," and regardless of the quality of your work, you can't help but feel that it is automatically superior to something done by a less experienced writer. Maybe you are older, and you've been plugging away at this book for years on end. As the senior member of your writing group, you act like the "boss" of everyone in it, especially younger writers, and you believe that your opinions are the correct ones. And of course, you believe that your book is automatically superior to one that only took a year to write. Or maybe you have a bunch of followers on Instagram, and you are fairly certain that this should translate into instant bestseller status.

Yes, effort, experience, and even internet fame often pay off in the long run. But it's not an automatic thing. You are not doing yourself a favor by believing that you are "owed" a bestseller.

I once had a writer reach out to me via email to ask me to read his work. I was a bit bemused as I had never heard from this person before, but I was curious, so I decided to engage.

"My book is up on Amazon, and I can't get anyone to review it," he wrote.

"Why don't you reach out to some of your readers-friends, or other people who have bought your book, and request a review," I suggested. "No one has bought it," was the reply.

Usually fail to sell a single copy is a factor of several things, including but not limited to lack of promotion, ugly cover, bad title… so I decided to look up this writer's book. He had the e-book listed at $25.99. $25.99? Maybe for a hardcover. Maybe for a coffee table book? But for an e-book with an amateur cover and a confusing title written by a virtual unknown? No way! When I brought this up with him in my next email, he gave me an answer that tested the limits of my ability to refrain from sarcasm: "It's well worth it, because my story is better than other stories." Hmm. Conversation over.

The pain of not gaining readers had allowed this writer to take a first step towards self-discovery, in reaching out to a writing coach, and now he had taken a few steps back. In this writer's case, I can see one of two outcomes:

-Either he will eventually grow so frustrated at his lack of success that he adopts true self-honesty to see where he's going wrong, and will take his head out of his ass for long enough to see where he's going wrong...

-Or he will become a frustrated creative who now will adopt the victim mentality because he feels that it is a more manageable pain for him. He might even start to blame me for refusing to review his book.

-Absolutes, all or nothing/Perfection

With this mindset, you believe that there is only one way to succeed as an author. There is only one kind of writing that is "good." There is only one way to publish a book. Also, if you don't have a specific level of education or a specific writing routing, you will never succeed. If you skip writing one day, or if you are stuck on something, or if your first few pages suck, you might as well give up, and if one agent doesn't want to represent you, you might as well quit. Your book will never be perfect and thus you will never be able to release it into the world... Better yet, you should not even insult the noble tradition of writing and you should give up now. If you're writing a work of historical fiction, you might need to get a PhD in the era

you're writing about just to be even somewhat worthy...
(Trust me, I've been there!) You use this mindset to self-sabotage your own progress, and/or you use it to become
the person everyone loves to hate: the self-unaware critic
who tries to poison everyone else with their
pronouncements.

I know a writer who loves to dole out advice. Here are
a few of her "gems":

-There is a short list of literary agents that are worth
anything.

-There are only a couple "real" publishing companies.

-If you don't get an advance of a certain size you
should take your book elsewhere.

-If you don't get your book into certain bookstores,
you aren't really an author.

-E-books? Forget those. They don't even count.

I have managed to keep this writer away from my
writing group, because, you guessed it, according to people
who have seen her in action in another group, she likes to
take over and spew out advice. God forbid she volunteers
to critique someone's work- if it's not highbrow literary
fiction, she'll thoroughly trash it.

Apparently, that writer hasn't gone to her writing group
in forever. Is it because she's so busy with her successful
writing career? Constantly off at book signings while
writing the follow-up to her highly acclaimed magnum
opus? Nope. I forgot to give you this one little detail: she's

never actually finished anything. Her perfectionism won't let her.

-Fixated on details

There are so many details that go into writing and publishing a book, and there is absolutely no question that you're going to fixate on one or several of them.

-Can't come up with the perfect name for a secondary character? It's going to block you and keep you from moving forward.

-Haven't even gotten midway through the writing process and already agonizing about which agent you will pitch to first? You are getting way ahead of yourself.

-Spending more time on a detailed "Bible" for your book, so much so that the darn thing is longer than your book should be? You're shooting yourself in the foot.

Maybe you are focusing on the details because you know there is something not right about the big picture. Like, oh, right… you haven't finished your book.

I'm not just being mean: I've been there. I have a collection of book covers that I reworked until they were perfect… for books I never finished. Therefore, it is easy for me to be sympathetic to the writers in my writing group who are paralyzed by the fear of making a mistake: is this historical detail accurate? Is that date correct? Is this the way you actually embalm a body? You know, that type of thing…

Being preoccupied with errors is a necessary evil, or not even an evil actually, as some errors can be serious. We've all seen companies that charge forward with projects without thinking of the ramifications and without concern for some of the less desirable effects of what they have put into play. As a fiction author, however, most of these fears don't apply. In your book, you could decide that marshmallows are toxic, and that becomes truth in your book. If you are writing from a place of kindness, and if you have the desire to make your writing as good as it can be, you can start now and then review the inevitable small errors further down the road, when you have a whole manuscript. Also, fixing errors is what second and third editions are for, and in e-books, this is a moot point: they can be corrected anytime.

- "I'm a creative!"

Why is this a limiting mindset? Once your brain has settled on what a creative should and shouldn't do, on how a creative is supposed to act, think, and work, you can fall into the trap of second guessing everything you do as a writer as not creative enough. The other problem with this is that many writers have a more deep-seated secret conviction that creativity does not yield a "real" job and that pursuing creative success (at least in a popularity/financial sense) is "selling out." Many would-be writers today hold conflicting beliefs: success equals money, but also true creatives don't care about money, only passion. This leads writers to avoid planning for success, because now success equals failure. Also, as a *creative*, you are probably a little solitary and misunderstood. No one understands your work as well as you do, so joining a writing group is futile. Also, you wouldn't even take any criticism as anything more than a pure personal attack, because, well, you're misunderstood.

These mindsets can lead to a very myopic vision of what writing a book is and isn't. Your work may end up appealing to a super restricted group of people, if you ever finish it under those huge pressures and convictions. Also, when you are a creative, and writing is a passion project, you run the risk of burning out because you expect your passion to feed you, unflagging. Your book may be also lacking in structure because you're expecting your passion to give you direction.

-Fear (of success *and* failure)

Failure puts your abilities into question. You have exposed yourself, and now you have failed in a public arena. When you have this mindset, you don't realize that so ridiculously few people that you know actually give a crap about what you are working on, not to mention that you were under no obligation to "put yourself out there" where your friends and family are concerned, until your book is so "out there" that they cannot fail to notice, and that in itself is success.

Fear of *success* is more insidious: writers are afraid to succeed because of all the things that will come with success: the extra work, the expectations, the need to promote yourself and your book. With the extra exposure of success comes the fear of exposure and looking ridiculous or uncool or foolish. This fear keeps a lot of writers not only from finishing their books, but also it keeps them writing stuff that is "normal," stuff that isn't "weird" and doesn't make waves. These fears and mindsets are often strengthened and compounded by "well meaning" friends and family, who seek to "protect you" from ridicule and failure. In reality, they are afraid that if you fail you will make them look bad by extension if they supported you. On the other hand, if you succeed beyond your wildest dreams, they may now be "inferior" to you. I blame this behavior for a phenomenon you may have noticed on social media: Post a photo of your dog or of your kids, or even a silly selfie, and you'll get lots of likes, compliments, and fawning comments. Post something about your work in progress or your finished book or an article you wrote… and it's crickets! And you know what? That's ok. Maybe it's the algorithm. Or maybe your friends and family are not your audience.

-Scarcity Mindset

With this mindset, you focus on the belief that there are a limited number of books that "make it," a limited amount of space in bookstores and libraries, and a limited number of readers on this earth, with limited time to read, and limited money to spend. Your chances of making it are incredibly slim, and any writer who succeeds is one who has taken one of the "spots" in the pantheon of successful writers, and they have hence stolen that spot from you.

Writing now becomes a contest, and you can't help but rank other writers compared to yourself. You would certainly not want to help out another writer, that would be self-defeating, right? In fact, if you're in a certain mood, you will get on social media and trash any writer that puts themselves out there. You also assume that all other writers feel the same way as you.

When I was seeking to understand the behavior of trolls on boards meant to be supporting writers, I noticed this negative behavior. I observed the bad behavior of writers who time and time again demonstrated extreme reluctance to give new writers a leg up. I was wondering why… after all, a rising tide lifts up all boats, doesn't it?

But it's human nature to protect our turf. Many authors seem to view other authors as competition, or as the enemy. They think that another author's success will take away from their own. They think that there are a limited number of spots to be filled by writers, so that they had better get ahead themselves rather than to let the other guy succeed.

Yes, it is true that there are certain limited resources in the publishing world. They are: budgets, paper, and space. Publishers cannot afford to publish and market more than a certain number of titles a year, and bookstores and libraries simply cannot stock more than a certain number of books. So, if getting traditionally published by one of the big publishing houses is your only benchmark for success, you may indeed find yourself in a position of fear and competition. However, even in this situation, there are unknown authors who make it each and every year, so it *is* possible.

I have come across some forums online where authors can anonymously abuse each other. They view this is something fun, as a way to blow off steam harmlessly. But I find this far from harmless. It perpetuates negativity, and it perpetuates the idea of other authors as our enemies rather than as our peers. You never know how your book will fit into the market, and whether it succeeds has absolutely nothing to do with whether you were cooperative or competitive with other others. Wouldn't it be nicer to have a community, rather than going it alone? I find that his mindset is incredibly hard to reverse in authors. It has become such a deeply entrenched habit that it literally defines the stereotype of the solitary author.

There are further problematic mindsets, but the ones above are the main ones. We've all been guilty of displaying symptoms of some of these mindsets, or all of them, but we *can* change.

How?

Be conscious of whether you have a tendency to act based on negative, problematic mindsets and try to reverse that behavior.

Easier said than done? Hey, even if you just start by trying to reverse behaviors, that constant practice will eventually make it easier. When I say "reverse," I'm being literal. Take the negative behavior and do the opposite. It's not more complicated than that.

Problematic thoughts/behavior	What to think/do instead
"Writing is hard. I'm suffering all the time."	"I am lucky to have the opportunity to pursue my passion and to keep learning and growing despite the hard times. I am a badass."
"Rejected again. Gatekeepers suck."	"This is a sign that I need to keep working on my craft and an opportunity to exercise my determination and resilience. Is there another way to come at this?"
Focusing on what you lack as a writer.	Look at what you have and what sets

	you apart. How do your perceived shortcomings make you more relatable?
Feeling unworthy of any success or recognition that comes your way.	Feeling thankful for any success or recognition that comes your way.
Acting like you are owed certain things.	Working hard to actually earn those things.
Using setbacks and rejection to justify quitting.	Filing these episodes away as fun anecdotes you can tell to inspire others when you encounter success.
Criticizing the work of other writers.	Learning from their mistakes, and when appropriate, helping them to improve upon their work, without trying to make it something it's not or trying to enforce your will on their work to "improve" it.

Fixating on details.	Focusing on the big picture.
Feeling solitary, lonesome, and misunderstood.	Seeking out community.
Tying your self-worth to others' opinion of you and to the reception you get either online or in the real world.	Doing your best and speaking your truth. Those opinions will mean little to you in the long run.
Expecting friends and family to support your writing career and being disappointed if they don't.	Being thankful if they do.
Getting upset when your Facebook post doesn't get as many likes as you would like.	Focusing on an authentic and powerful message and then going after a more engaged audience for your work.
Agonizing over another writer's success.	Seeing others' success as proof that it is possible and using it as a blueprint.
Seeing other authors as competition.	Seeing other writers as friends and

	allies who know what you are going through.

OK, wait a second: It's not so easy to just swap one feeling for another, one behavior for another, is it? First of all, you need to get motivated to shift problem mindsets.

Why is it so imperative to shift negative mindsets?

-If you have the wrong mindset, everything becomes a struggle

Not because of the intrinsic difficulty of doing those things, but because of your perception and hence your reaction.

-Measuring yourself by your failure is a surefire way to fail further

That's because we tend to go towards the thing we are fixated on.

-Fixed mindsets prevent us from growing and improving

This is literally their definition.

-Fixed, problem mindsets can literally sap our happiness and our sense of achievement

The great news about mindset, as opposed to skills, artistic or physical performance, or knowledge, is that mindsets can be shifted drastically in moments. In a single sitting, you are capable of radically changing how you think and what you believe, and this will motivate you more than anything you've tried before.

Soon, you'll be able to swap the thought patterns and behaviors as listed above like a pro… we're going to give you the *skills* to do it.

SKILL 1: Reframe the issue

Rather than using words like *always* and *never*, which are a sign that you are making blanket pronouncements about yourself, your beliefs, your talents, your weaknesses, or those of others, you can reframe these concepts.

You probably need to see an example of this in action to see how it works:

Instead of:

- "I never manage to finish a book," try saying: "Until now, I've not been able to finish a book."

With a small shift in language, we are removing the absolute quality of the statement, and putting the statement in the past, so as to remove the assumption that we expect this situation to persist.

Instead of:

- "I could never join a writing group," try: "I haven't yet convinced myself to join a writing group."

Here, we are again removing the absolute nature of the statement and putting the power firmly with ourselves. It is up to us to convince ourselves to do something. It is in our power.

Instead of:

- "Other writers are often really rude and condescending," Try saying: "Sometimes, other writers have said things that I found rude and condescending."

Here, we are reframing the issue so that it is our reaction to others' behavior that is in question. We can always change our reaction even if we cannot change others' behavior. Notice how the statement is in the *past tense*. If you decide not to pay attention to rude or condescending behavior from here on in, that is absolutely in your power.

Instead of:

- "I suck at making outlines," try something like: "I'm still working on lessening my anxiety over outlines."

This transformation knowledges that anxiety is possible, however, it reframes it as something that can be reduced by the one who suffers it. It's reframed as a work in progress. It removes the direct correlation between outlines and failure and recognizes that failing at creating a good outline results in a painful feeling: anxiety, which can be managed.

Instead of:

- "I completely lack motivation," try "I tend to lack motivation, and it's therefore hard for me to push a project to completion."

Here, we remove the absolute nature of the statement, chalk it up to a tendency, and explain what in particular makes us come to that conclusion. Seeing if that the difficulty of pushing a project to completion is the issue, we can move to fix that rather than fixing a whole personality trait.

Instead of:

- "I don't have time to write," try "I'm realizing that making time to write could be an important priority for me."

Here, the blanket statement that is obviously not true is replaced by a realization about one's priorities, and the understanding that being honest about a situation is the first step in resolving it. It's all about priorities.

Do you see the pattern?

To reframe an issue, you:

-Tell the story in the **past tense**, as if acknowledging that the changes coming, removing the idea that you expect this to happen time and time again.

-Portray obstacles as things that are **a result of a behavior pattern** of yours rather than as something absolutely that can never be changed.

-Purposely **distance** yourself from the concepts and thoughts that are creating a blockage and frustration for you, even if it is purely linguistic for now.

Exercise:

On a sheet of paper, allow yourself to write down all of your worst, ugliest, most shameful beliefs. Use the prompts below for inspiration.

-About your talent as an author:

-About your work ethic:

-About your knowledge of writing and publishing:

-About who supports you:

-About the everyday process of writing:

-About when you get stuck:

-About your attempts to finish/publish a book:

-About your view of other writers:

-About the things keeping you from writing:

-About your chances for success:

Next, **reframe** these statements on a **separate** piece of paper.

Now, take the paper with the negative stuff on it, burn it, and flush the ashes down the toilet.

You're going to use the second sheet of paper, with the positive thoughts, as your own personal mantras, to reread when you're feeling "less than."

OK, are the crappy beliefs in the toilet, where they belong? Seriously, if you thought I was just being metaphorical, I wasn't.

Do it. Burn the paper and flush it down the toilet. It's part of The Spalmorum Method. You bought this book, you might as well be all in.

Congratulations!

You have literally just gotten rid of your crappy mindsets.

Don't let them define you anymore. Those fixed mindsets hurt. They made you believe that everything about you is carved in stone. They fed your anxiety, they provoked a need to prove yourself constantly, and they fostered a sense of competition with others based on fixed characteristics and a constant fear of being deficient, without a way of being able to fix it. You felt judged, you felt that every single piece of work you produced was an opportunity to take you down, to make you feel less than. Everything was setting you up for rejection by others who are "better."

Proving yourself takes a lot of energy, and this is energy not well spent. If you simply adopt the belief that you can improve on your basic qualities and keep growing, you will see that you are different from others, but no better or worse, and you can begin to strive for the things that are actually important to you rather than for acceptance and superiority.

Rather than wasting time trying not to fail, you will instead spend your time wisely trying to grow. Obviously, this is a much healthier mindset for a writer. It is taking the ego out of the writing process, and it is key.

Remember this:

Living in fear of what others think of you hurts. Not worrying about other's judgement is a much more comfortable way to go about your creative life. But also, the way you treat yourself and judge yourself and others teaches others how to treat you and judge you.

Now that you're well motivated to get rid of the damaging mindsets, here is a questionnaire to help you develop the radical but non-judgmental self-honesty that will free you up to start making room for positive, helpful mindsets. Notice that these questions are not meant to elicit negative blanket statements that bring the bad mindset right back in. View your shortcomings as though they belonged to a beloved child.

1) Which weaknesses have blocked you from writing success in the past? Are there concrete steps that you can take to improve on those?

2) What have been your worst failures when it comes to writing? How did they make you feel? Did they actually matter in the greater scheme of things? What did you learn from them?

3) What about the writing process do you enjoy most? What do you enjoy least? Why? Is there a way to make the things you enjoy least more enjoyable?

4) What is your goal in writing? What is your purpose? Is there something beyond celebrity, or showing others that you could do it? How can you better embrace that higher purpose?

5) Do you have a writing community? If not, why not? If you had one and left it, why? Might you be able to create the type of writing community that you wish for?

Now, here are some important thoughts and attitude tweaks, for when you're feeling the pain of writer's block brought on by fixed mindset:

Feeling imperfect and less than?

At least you have standards! At least your ego doesn't give you an overinflated sense of self. You can always improve. Always.

Having an overly hard time doing something or learning something? Feeling painfully stupid?

Hey, you're ahead because you are actually trying to learn something- the majority of people in this world don't even have that level of intellectual curiosity! Why not brainstorm on how you could set yourself up differently? Are there other tactics that you did not think of? Is there a reason for your resistance? As the writer Ryan Holiday has pointed out, "the obstacle is the way." Or is there a way of skipping over that task in some way that will not impact your overall project negatively?

Dwelling on your past failures? Feeling the pain of failure over and over again?

Failure doesn't just happen. Whether it was your fault, or someone else's fault, it happened for a reason. Find that reason. The *real* reason, not a whitewashed version of the facts that is more comfortable for you. Lean into the disappointment. Why not examine how your failures became or can still become learning opportunities? If they did not become a learning opportunity at the time, there is still time to learn from them now.

Stuck seeking approval?

Why do you need approval from others, when you know what your capabilities, intentions, and goals are best of all? Seeking approval from others who are not coming from the same place is silly. If anything, their approval will be superficial, just like any disapproval they might have, because they do not know where you're coming from, no matter how well they know you. Seeking approval is a waste of time and energy, because approval becomes like a drug: the minute the approval stops, disappears, or lessens, the pain comes back twofold.

Are you frustrated with how long it's taking you to get from where you are to where you want to be?

Learn to look at the growth you are undergoing, the progress you are making, and savor the journey rather than being impatient. This journey is adding so much to your end product. See this period as paying your dues. Know that things *always* take longer than we think it will. Underestimating the time and effort a task will take to complete is something that literally all humans do. It's called a "planning fallacy," and it's been studied extensively. Maybe it's a psychological trick to ensure that we keep launching projects rather than getting discouraged by the amount of time it will take.

But I challenge you to give yourself a buffer on the time it will take you to write your book: How long do you think it will take you to do a rough draft? Now revise that amount of time by imagining that there are going to be a few obstacles thrown in your way: an illness, a work project, travel, lack of inspiration, an out of town visitor.

Now multiply that time by two. Write this time down. Now do the same thing for how long it will take you to revise and edit this rough draft, how long it will take you to create a submission package, etc. No matter how long it takes you to finish this book and have it published, you are still moving forward. If you are moving forward, you are better off than you were the day before each and every day when it comes to being a writer. Think about that. It's incredible. You can't always say that about another day job.

Seeing others as competition?

If you're valuing the process and the art and the greater purpose of what you're doing, you will be happy to share it with others at all stages of your project. If you feel confident in yourself, you won't be afraid of someone judging you or stealing ideas, because you'll know that you are unique. Others can be a great support, but you should not count on them or lean on them too heavily. This is about depending on yourself.

Feeling the effects of imposter syndrome? That you're "not a real writer"?

What's a real writer? I've interacted with a bunch of writers, read and watch interviews with a bunch of authors, and other than the fact that they write, and that they are passionate about writing, I can't really put my finger on other commonalities that make them more "real" than you. On the contrary, writers are a pretty darn diverse bunch. Abandon what you think a writer is supposed to be like, what do you think they're supposed to sound like, look like, and dress like. Abandon those ideas of how old you should've been when you published your first award winning novel. The idea that you even need to win an award. The image of what you think something should be like is just another level of pressure that is unrealistic and unneeded. Once you do the work to be a writer, you will be a writer, and that will be what a real writer looks like. According to Steven Pressfield, "If you find yourself asking yourself (and your friends), "Am I really a writer? Am I really an artist?" chances are you are. The counterfeit innovator is wildly self-confident. The real one is scared to death."

Wondering when you will arrive at the "finish line"? Feeling the pain of the unknown?

So many writers run into trouble because there are significant gaps in their goals: there is the goal of the finished novel, and there is the fantasy of the best-selling author: that idealized image of themselves at a book signing, Champagne flute in one hand, fountain pen in the other, autographing books for adoring fans. There's nothing before the finished book, there is nothing between that and the life of fame and luxury, and there is nothing after that fabulous book signing. The vaguer the goal, the less straightforward the steps you must take to get there.

When is it enough? When will you feel that you have "arrived"? Unless you are one of the lucky few who find a spot on the NYT bestsellers list, or win a big award, or have your book made into a movie, the goal seems to be a moving, nebulous target.

Here's the workaround: make tiny goals, make huge goals. Make "attainable" goals and "reach" goals. Make vision boards and be prepared to attain some goals and to fall short of others. Be prepared for new goals to materialize. Just because you've achieved one goal doesn't mean that that's enough. Even if you're amazed that you have achieved something far beyond what you thought you might, keep making goals. Keep challenging yourself. Once you achieve what you thought was your main goal, you will see that you have no limits and that you can keep yourself excited and motivated and do more than you ever thought. That is a wonderful idea, isn't it?

After all of this, do the perceived obstacles standing in your way still seem insurmountable? Do you still have no time & energy for writing? Are you still feeling the pain of writer's block and success block, with no sense of possibility and no reprieve?

Ok, first step: stop being a drama queen.

I'm not being glib. Some of us live for the drama, and it's not helping. Remember radical self-honesty? It's important.

In addition to writing groups, I host Creative Happy Hours as an offshoot of my Creative Happy Hour podcast. These happen in the evening, either at a local wine bar or at someone's home. Many attendees are writers, but I also have chefs, painters, musicians, architects, screenwriters, scientists, dancers, and designers. Usually, these meetings result in people expressing a desire to try another creative means of expression, or describing a project they dream of, often writing related.

On a recent one of these evenings, at my home, I had a new person, a friend of a friend, show up. I'll call her Nina. Nina was young and charming, and quickly had the other creatives eating out of her hands as she regaled them with tales of her fascinating life experiences. It was obvious from her natural storytelling ability that Nina was naturally talented, and her youth led me to believe that she would have a great aptitude for learning whatever was lacking. However, she started raising objections for why she would never be able to succeed. None of these reasons were anything I hadn't heard before a thousand times. The other writers in the group were also familiar with these excuses, and gently reassured Nina, and encouraged her.

But the more they tried to be positive and reassuring, the more Nina pushed back. No! She would not succeed! There were too many obstacles stacked against her!

She was displaying every symptom of the victim mindset. Eventually, I noticed that Nina was not really listening to any of the guidance and support we were trying to give her. She was too blocked.

If you're like Nina, if you skimmed over the previous paragraphs without really absorbing them because you decided they were a crock of bullshit and wouldn't help you because you're too far gone and super special and unique in your writer's block, take a step back. Take a deep breath.

I'm saying this in love and kindness:

You're not that special.

I mean, you *are* special, of course you are. But you are not special in your writer's block. I have seen so many of these objections and blocks before. If you're reading this book, you are at least conscious that your blocks are causing you pain. So, do yourself a favor: re-read the book and pay attention this time. Give yourself the gift of fixing what's broken. Be kind to yourself and allow yourself to do the thing you're passionate about, the thing that feeds your dreams and your soul.

Be realistic. Do you still truly believe you are uniquely lacking in ability, time, or concentration, or any other thing that would enable you to reach the goals that you have set up for yourself? Try to remember that there are world-famous, bestselling authors who were mentally ill, homeless, in jail, or political refugees. Hopefully that's not you. But even if it is you, let those authors be proof that even then, success is possible.

There's a possibility that you do need a break: some time away to reassess your goals and the current situation, to create a game plan, to build a stronger foundation, and then to come back at your goals refreshed, perhaps from a slightly or radically different angle than before.

The concept of time is very fluid, and none of us have a deadline when it comes to our ultimate creative production, unless of course, we have a deadline from our editor or publisher, and that would be a very good thing, right?

Chapter 7: 3 Magic Tools for Writing Success

Now that you know more about how mindset works, and that you are a little clearer on how to adopt the correct mindsets that will work for you, let's get even deeper into *applying* this knowledge. You can have adopted all the right mindsets, or so you think, yet still not be putting them into *action* in a way that is going to move you forward.

Whether you are a fiction writer, a memoirist, a filmmaker, a content writer, a journalist, or a marketer, or you are using storytelling for a powerful other project, our mindset changes are like magic tools that will give you newfound confidence and power that are guaranteed to lead to increased success.

All of these new mindsets boil down to "attitude." And attitude is just *one* of three "magic tools" in the successful author's arsenal. Mindset alone will only take you so far.

The 3 magic tools for writing success:

1) **Attitude**
2) **Accountability**
3) **Action**

What? That's it? Those are the magic tools? Yes, they sound simple, but they're actually super powerful. They're the three pillars of success, and they all work together. You can't leave out any of the ingredients or the alchemy won't work. Let me explain.

Attitude

The first magic tool for success: the right attitude.

The correct mindsets we established in the previous chapter all come together to form the right *attitude*. But you didn't actually believe it was going to be that easy, did you? Mindset is just part of developing the correct attitude for success, and attitude is just one of the ingredients for success.

You can adopt a bunch of positive mindsets and still feel like you have writer's block, and still not finish your book.

Because sometimes, all these great new mindsets fade away... old habits come back.

In this section, I will give you ideas to "top up" your mindset so that you maintain an overall positive attitude.

Attitude problem: Lack of motivation.

Look, I'm not going to motivate you to write.

You can't actually motivate people. All one can do is to ensure that people are internally motivated, and then spend time creating an environment in which they can excel. That is what a good writing group does.

You cannot be motivated if you can't see what it is you want to do. What if you vaguely think you want to be a writer, but you can't motivate? It takes thinking to make a plan, but it makes *feeling* to make that plan into action. This is where leaning into the pain of not finishing your book comes in. You need to *feel* that writing is important, that getting your book out there is what will ease the pain. No pain? Gain seems highly unlikely.

In terms of motivation, here is the number one thing that you can do: you've all heard the rule about writing a certain amount each and every day, no exceptions. That's great, but maybe it's something you need to work up to. Instead, each day, remind yourself of *why* you are doing this. Why you want it. Do something each day to get further than you were yesterday. Celebrate small successes. Celebrate your progress.

I've mentioned multiple times that motivation is hard when you can't clearly see your goal. If you don't know exactly what you want from your writing, you can't work towards it. You probably guessed it from the fact that I firmly believe that writer's block is a much broader issue than simply coming up with plot points. Embarking on a writing project is not just about coming up with a story. A story is a great jumping-off point, but it's not enough. If you don't go into writing knowing who your audience will be and how you will promote your book, you are already at a disadvantage. Think about it this way: you may have a GPS, but if you don't have the address of where you're going, it can't help you.

Now is the time to be honest with yourself: think back to *why* you've wanted to be a writer for a long time and to what success as an author means for you, personally.

Answering these questions will help you to see more clearly:

-What kind of books do you like to read?

-What is it that you like about them?

-Is this the kind of book you would like to write?

-What is standing in the way of you writing a book like that?

-You've written a book- How do you feel when you finish writing it?

-How do you describe it to your friends?

-How does the cover look?

-What are your greatest hopes for this book?

-Who is your ideal reader?

-How do you want your book to make people feel?

-How many readers would you ideally have?

-Do you want to make money from this book?

-If so, are you willing to work hard to promote it? (i.e., do something that is more business than writing)

-Do you want a conventional publishing deal?

-If so, are you willing to work on the submission package and face possible rejection, and if it is accepted, play the waiting game?

-How will you feel if you never write this book?

-What does success as a writer mean to *you*? (Do you really want to be a **writer**, or do you want the fantasy accoutrements of the bestselling author's lifestyle? Fame? Money? Book tours that take you to glamorous places? Book signings full of clamoring fans?)

Attitude problem: Fear of failure.

Why do we keep bringing up fear of failure? Haven't we already discussed it to death in the mindset section? I mention it again because this is truly one of the hardest things to shake.

But really: why do you think failure will hurt so much? The worst that could happen is that you would be right back where you are now. Wait, that's not true: you would be much better off than where you are now- you would have a book or at least part of a book to show for your efforts. You would have learned from the experience and be in a better position to start again.

I have had so many failures on my road to writing success that I could write a whole book about it. And I don't regret any of it. Frankly, the biggest failure would be not having been true to yourself and to your dreams. In fact, that is the top regret expressed by people on their death beds. Don't let this be you. It is not too late. But it is *not* true to say that it is *never* too late.

Also, this is important: writing and publishing are uniquely rejection-filled fields. You will realize that your worth as a writer cannot be tied to the opinions of a gatekeeper or two or ten.

Rejection only hurts if you let it.

You will understand that so many rejections happen because the great majority of people in the publishing industry are driven by how much they think they can make from your book and not always by how good your story is or isn't. However, do keep in mind that if your story is undeniably awesome, agents and publishers should be able to realize that they can profit from it.

Again, what does success mean for you? Is it writing your story to the best of your ability and getting it out there by any means necessary? Or are you dreaming of a conventional publishing contract, and of lots and lots of money? Either route is possible, but you need to decide what drives you, and if you've developed the right attitude, you will identify the things that need to happen for your success, and make them happen, regardless of time, difficulty, and obstacles.

Attitude problem: Impatience and lack of perseverance.

You say you really want to be a writer, but you're discouraged that it will take so long. You don't have that kind of time. Several months to a year or even more to write a first draft? No thank you! You're busy! Spending many hours, days, and weeks on edits and rewrites? Whaaat? Ain't nobody got time for that! And even worse, you've heard that agents take their sweet time getting to your precious manuscript, and if you get a publishing deal, it might be two years before your book even comes out? You want it all to happen *now*. Or else, why waste your time?

Be honest, what were you doing until now? Probably a lot of time-wasting stuff. You can keep doing that while you wait. Or, if you really are a writer, you can be working on improving your skills, and on other writing projects, including your next book, and on building your author's platform, and on supporting other writers because of your love of writing.

In fact, you can be so busy being a writer that you won't even notice the time going by. If you love writing, anything that involves writing is not a waste of time.

Attitude problem: Letting your lack of skills/knowledge stop you.

You feel that your current education makes you somehow "less than." Some of the most powerful and artistic books written were produced by people with little formal education, and conversely, many best-sellers are widely considered to be badly written from an academic standpoint.

Every time I post something off the cuff on social media, there is at least one person who will correct my grammar. Guys, I have a PhD, and sometimes I make a glaring mistake. And sometimes, these "editors" are actually "correcting" perfectly fine casual, colloquial lingo perfectly suited to Facebook into formal Queen's English (God forbid I should leave a preposition dangling in an Instagram post!). Whenever this happens, I will look that person up, eager to know what they have done with their perfect grasp of grammar and sentence structure. Unfortunately, it's usually a whole bunch of nothing. These critics are not even of any use to me or to others as an editor, because they don't understand style and context. It's a bummer. But it's their problem, not yours! Anyone who lords their grammar over you is not a constructive person to have around. They are displaying some type of pain brought on by their ego and a not-so-secret inferiority complex.

What's more, everyone is capable of further educating themselves and hiring or enlisting someone to help whip their writing into shape. You don't need to pay $30,000 for an MFA in creative writing or pay thousands for an editor before you're ready. There are many other ways of improving your writing skills, including tools on the Spalmorum website and other free information that is readily available all over the Internet, if you're willing to look for it and sift through it.

Being a writer means being a lifelong learner, remember? We are all simply on a different spot on the sliding scale of education, talent, and ability. Many times, an increase in determination and perseverance can more than make up for a possible deficiency in education or ability. Also, keep in mind that not all readers are Nobel laureates or in possession of genius level intelligence. Your writing will find a reader, or a whole lot of readers, with whom your words and ideas and story resonate, and isn't that the point?

Some would-be writers are tripped up by the fact that they "don't know how" to write and publish a book. But anyone can learn that, if they actually care to. It often baffles me that so many people who claim to want to be writers don't seem to know how to read or listen. If you actually read or listen to and act on all of the information about writing and a writing career available to you: grammar rules, necessary steps, advice from professionals, directions, advice, and feedback from agents and publishers, etc. you will get further than you ever thought possible.

Often, on online writing forums, I'll notice would-be authors stating that they hope to make lots of money from their writing, and then asking a basic question that proves that a) they haven't even started writing, b) they haven't educated themselves as to the basic process c) they haven't read any of the other threads on that forum because their question has already been answered a thousand times. Oh, and d) their grammar sucks. Sorry, that was a low blow, but it's warranted here, I promise.

The long and the short of it is, if writing is important to you, you will stop wasting time asking stupid questions, and get smart about getting the answers and skills you need.

Attitude problem: succumbing to fear and doubt.

This may stem from your own perfectionism, i.e., being afraid your work will never be good enough, or from fear of negative or doubting feedback from friends and family. According to them, they're trying to spare you from a life of poverty, rejection, and frustration by "helpfully" pointing out that your chances of being published are slim, or that they've never thought of you as a writer, so you must therefore not be one, etc. etc. However, these people are usually not your audience, and many times, they are projecting their own fears, pains, or frustrations onto you. Maybe they're secretly frustrated "aspiring writers" too, but they never got brave enough and committed enough to progress beyond that. Don't worry about them. Thank them for their "support" and move on. And stop beating yourself up about how bad your writing is. I'm not saying you shouldn't keep trying to be as good as you can be, or that you should ignore constructive criticism from those who are actually in the business of writing. The sooner you realize that you are not actually your own worst critic and that a practiced eye can vastly improve your manuscript, the better off you'll be.

By the way, according to a recent study conducted at King's College in London, there's a link between worrying a lot and verbal intelligence. People with a heightened tendency to generate negative thoughts are more likely to have a highly active imagination. So congrats, worrywart: you may actually be a better writer than you give yourself credit for. (Yikes, there's a dangling preposition…the horror!)

Attitude problem: Believing that your laziness is your fatal flaw and that you can't do anything about it:

This is where the tough love comes in: tons of people have ideas. A tiny percentage of those people will do anything about it, whether it's in business, in writing, or in any other realm. I cringe when I hear an umpteenth person tell me about how creative they are, and how people should pay them for their marvelous ideas so that they can make money without going through the boring part, which is the execution, which "anyone can do." I always crack up when a writer or would-be entrepreneur is "afraid someone will steal their idea." If the "thief" is committed enough to fall in love with that idea, so much so that they stick with it and do the work that goes into writing and publishing a 300 page book based on this idea before you start or finish your own book, you should be impressed by the "thief" and disappointed in yourself.

Yes, writing is hard. Still, thinking writing is *too* hard at this juncture, after having read this much of this book, might be the one reason you actually should quit. You should know it's hard, but still *need* to do it. If that's not the case, writing might not be for you right now. That's not to say it won't eventually be for you, later. Why don't you give it a break for a while and circle back if your story is still calling to you? But if you're still reading this, I don't think you're a quitter.

And don't think that laziness is an easy alternative to action, either. There are several people, including but not limited to writers, who have admitted to me that they are mortified at how lazy they are, but that they feel they can't do anything about it. Their laziness, they tell me, is like a physical force that keeps them immobile, in bed, or on the couch. It makes them procrastinate, not sometimes, but always. These people are not describing that fun, occasional laziness that can see you hanging out with a loved one, bingeing on Netflix and enjoying every minute of it, or choosing to stay in bed an extra hour rather than going to class or working out. No. This is long-term, profound laziness. These people's friends and families will make uneasy jokes about it, or they'll try to snap them out of it. They'll try to use reason, or threats, or begging, but none of that can shift it. They think the lazy person is taking the easy way out, but they're not. They're in pain. The knowledge that they feel absolutely incapable of doing the things they are expected to do, want to do, or know they should do, is acutely embarrassing.

This is not just laziness. It's depression. If you think you may be depressed, there is no shame in it: seek help. You don't need to feel this way. You can be so much better. Your chances of writing your book will exponentially increase. This kind of pain is not a prerequisite to be a "real" author. But again, if you feel that pain, please, please take it as what it is: a sign that something needs to change. Once you have dealt with the clinical angle, we can get back to run-of-the-mill laziness which is just lack of priorities, work ethic, or motivation.

Here are the top actionable tips and tricks to get the attitude and mindset needed to be a successful author:

-Redefine success

Success need not be an absolute notion. You get to decide what success means to you and celebrate that when it happens. Focus on the small victories that take you closer to that final vision.

-Stop making excuses

Accept that you are the responsible for your own success- and your own failures. Luck has little to do with it, and no one is going to be successful for you.

-Give yourself permission to fail and fail again

What if you do fall on your face? What's the worst that could happen? Failure can't hurt you any more than you allow. Your manuscript got rejected by an agent? Wow! You completed a manuscript and followed through with submitting it? What can you do to get you closer to succeeding next time? Make sure there is a next time.

-Don't quit

Transforming your mindset is not easy. It won't happen all at once. You'll have setbacks. But consistently striving towards it will bring you closer to success than anything else possibly could. It takes an everyday effort, and lots of reminders.

-Come up with a mantra

You can whip out this mantra when you're feeling weak. "I'm doing this," or "I'm a better writer each day" or "always learning" are good starts, but you can come up with something that speaks to you personally. Bring out that sheet of paper with your revised mindsets on it.

These "actionable" tips are a great transition to the next pillar of success, **ACTION**.

Action

Action is the difference between wishing and doing, between success and failure.

Let me tell you about a couple of writers I know.

Susie (not her real name) is a vivacious and creative friend of mine. She lives in LA, which is, as you may know, the writing town to end all writing towns. One night, she was lucky enough to bump into a well-regarded and well-connected producer at a party. She told him about a script she was "working on-" really, it was more of an idea at that stage, but her idea was really pretty good, and she described it in her trademark enthusiastic way, so it garnered interest from the producer, who was intrigued enough by the concept to consider making it into a TV pilot. He gave my friend a timeframe in which to produce a full pitch package. This was to include a "more polished" version of the script (ha!), full character descriptions, and a synopsis. The producer told my friend he would present this package to other Hollywood executives he knew.

Did my friend even realize how lucky she was? Not only had she met and impressed a powerful person, but she had them on her side. If she just carried out her part of the deal, he was going to use his pull to get her idea in front of people who counted. She also had another huge advantage, which she didn't see as an advantage at the time: a specific timeframe, which gave her a built-in deadline.

I believe that a deadline is one of the most motivating things there is, but Susie didn't see it that way. She panicked. For two weeks, I called her every day. I wanted to help her by providing accountability. But she said it was just stressing her out. In fact, the thought of potentially disappointing the producer was stressing her out so much, she explained, that she absolutely needed to distract herself with a million things that weren't writing. Here's one of our phone calls:

"What are you doing now?" I asked.

"Shopping for shoes to wear when I have my next meeting with the producer."

"You aren't gonna have a meeting if you continue like this," I warned.

"Don't worry," she said. "I have it all in my head. It won't take me long to get it done. I just need to relax."

Poor Susie. If it was so easy to relax and get the cool things that are in our heads onto paper, in usable form, we would all be bestselling authors! Needless to say, my friend didn't get her pitch done. She burned her bridges with that producer by wasting his time. She returned the shoes. And she's still talking about her "dream" of being a writer. She refuses to see that if it hadn't been for her laziness and probably her fear of failure, she would probably be a successful writer right now, with perhaps a TV show or at the very least valuable experience and exposure under her belt.

Not acting leads to failure no matter how lucky and talented you are.

Another person I met in LA, Jane, doesn't have the natural charm that Susie possesses, and certainly isn't the type to go to industry parties. Unlike Susie, even though Jane at least tried to write a little every day, she wasn't that confident of her skills. She'd been trying to move her novel along, but not really getting anywhere because of self-doubt and lack of support.

When picking up bagels one morning, Jane came across a sign announcing a writers' meetup group. The format was low-pressure: meet in the bagel shop one evening a week, grab a snack or a glass of wine, work uninterrupted for an hour or two, and then discuss one's work, or even read it, to the other writers there. Now, Susie wouldn't have even considered joining a writing group that meets at a bagel shop. That's just not what "cool" writers do, is it? But for Jane, it was the sort of low pressure, social environment she realized she'd been missing. Jane started attending the group and making it a priority. Just by coming to this writers' group, Jane had transitioned from aspiring writer, to real writer. The more she showed up, the more others seemed to consider her as a writer. The simple act of telling someone "I can't have dinner with you on Monday, I have writers' group," made her sound like a professional, one for whom writing is a priority. Jane literally had tears in her eyes when she told me about the first time someone introduced her as a writer. Soon, Jane was shopping her manuscript around to agents, several of which she was referred to by other writers in the group. And she was offered a publishing deal. Nothing with a six-figure advance, but an opportunity to have her book published and discovered by her audience.

It took a single action for Jane to transition from "aspiring" to "real" writer, especially in her mind, which is what counts. And now, of course, all of her actions support that.

When you keep *acting* to move forward, you will sooner or later move forward, and the effect only intensifies over time.

Now that you know the importance of action, what are some of the small actions you can take right now to further your career as a writer? Which simple actions can get you closer to being an author? You might think you don't have time. I've broken this down into things that you can do in a minute, five minutes, or an hour.

Actions for when you have a minute:

-Tweet something about writing.
-Like 10 writer's posts on Instagram and comment on one.
-Follow 10 other writers on Insta or FB.
-Add some useful tasks to your to do list.
-Tackle some of the quick tasks on your list.
-Answer that email that's sitting in your inbox.
-Delete some emails.
-Sign up for a newsletter about writing/publishing.
- Back up your computer/save your work in progress to an external drive.

Actions for when you have 5 minutes:

- Post on your author Instagram account
- Dash off a paragraph.
-Jot down some ideas/brainstorm.
- Read an article on punctuation.
-Ask a question on a writing board on Facebook.
-Enter writing goals and deadlines into your calendar.
-Do a quick administrative task that is hanging over your head.
-Describe your reader avatar.

-Write a synopsis of your book. (This is harder than writing a whole chapter so you can do this repeatedly)

-Figure out your persona.

-Tweak your tagline.

-Read an article about writing/publishing.

Actions for when you have an hour or two:

- Attend a writers' group or event.

-Research your genre or your niche.

-Write a blog post.

-Review a book.

-Reread your character/location bible.

-Update your website/your social media profiles.

-Compile a list of possible outlets to market your book to.

-Research agents and publishers.

-Develop a look and feel for your online presence.

-Research 'real world" networking opportunities for writers.

-Design and order business cards.

-Creative an editorial calendar.

-Create a list of 20 websites that accept guest posts.

Make sure to plan for the tasks that you plan to achieve and cross them off of your to-do list as a record of how much you've done. When you've decided to start a new task or project that is important to you, announce it somewhere so that it can be seen by others. When you make measurable progress, celebrate it. Why? Because of the third pillar of success: Accountability.

Accountability

It's human nature: we get more done if we join a group or a class, or report back to a coach, or announce our intention to do something in a public forum. We feel obligated, and supported, and we don't want to fail in front of others (though seriously, there's no shame in failing- just pick yourself up and try again). Remember the example I gave you of Jane, who joined a writing group and kicked off the events that led to her book deal? That's the power of accountability. Though of course Action and Attitude came into play too. Keep in mind that accountability does not work as well at all if you don't already have the inner motivation. Accountability is mostly for helping people who possess the motivation but whose resolve is flagging, or who are hitting a bumpy patch.

Having writer friends can keep you writing. Having writer enemies can keep you writing, too. If the definition of a writer is someone who writes, and if you're getting distracted and not doing that, you can get away from your purpose without even realizing it. And then, are you really a writer? Writing is a pretty solitary pursuit. You don't often get positive affirmations unless you go looking for them. It can be hard to keep going, day after day, paragraph after paragraph, draft after draft, without support. That's another good part of having a writing community.

What if there are no other writers in your area?

I live part of the year in a *very* rural environment. You know what? The minute I started looking, I realized that there were quite a few authors around, and several writing groups already in existence, as well as interest expressed to form yet another at the local art center. The more "boring" and "quiet" your town, the more people will jump at the chance to attend a writing group if you start one. And if meeting in person is absolutely out of the question, there are other options.

Don't sabotage yourself by assuming that all writing support needs to come from a group of "cool" and "successful" novelists with a few published bestsellers under their belts, who meet in a trendy coffee shop with artisanal pour-overs.

A writer's group can be:

-2 or 3 moms meeting in each other's homes after school drop-off once a week for support and advice.

-A class at your local college or Y or public library that includes instruction and critique.

-A lunchtime writing group in your office.

-A small to medium sized group of busy people who commit to regular meetings, where a moderator keeps the discussion targeted and helpful.

-A regular Skype session and document sharing with another writer whose work complements yours or speaks to you.

-A larger, more fluid group that people attend when they are able for writing and voluntary critique. One person "leads" and acts as organizer.

-2 or 3 or 4 full time writers spending multiple hours of each day in a co-working space for creatives and discussing issues over lunch or coffee.

-A focused online forum with regular members who commit to positive critique and don't allow trolling or bullying- you can easily start your own on Facebook or join an existing one.

And if you don't have time to join a writing group or do any of those activities, even once a month? Then you aren't prioritizing your writing. Changing your mindset also means opening your eyes to the excuses you are using to explain why you aren't doing what you claim to be your dream, so that you can eliminate them.

-Too busy raising your kids to join a writing group?

Have your partner support you by watching the kids while you attend an evening group or join an online group that you can participate in while the kids play or nap.

-Too busy at work?

If you're literally working 24/7, you're a robot and probably don't need to be reading this, plus with advances in AI you will soon be able to multitask enough to write a bestseller every day. Otherwise, you can carve out time to seek out accountability. *If it's important to you.* How about finding other writers at work who will join a lunchtime or happy hour writing group? Your excuses are just excuses.

"If Voltaire and Marquis de Sade could write in prison, then you can do it in suburbia, at lunch, at work, or after your kids go to sleep. You will always find excuses if you want them and you probably do."- Scott Berkun

So that's it- that's the secret:

1) Attitude
2) Accountability
3) Action

Take time to focus on what these *really* mean. Most people will take a piece of advice and never actually stop to think what it truly entails, let alone follow that advice to the letter.

I was watching a Master Class by the legendary R&B artist Usher, who was teaching people how to perform. His advice boiled down to:

"Do your best."

At first, I scoffed at this. How trite. He'd really dialed it in, hadn't he?

And then I really thought about it. It was brilliant advice. *Magical*, even. But of all the people who watched that Master Class, I doubt that many, if any, actually fully acted on that advice.

And that's why Usher is Usher, and everyone else is still sitting there watching other people succeed over and over instead of changing their losing mindset and getting out there and actually doing their *best*.

Same goes to you. If you *truly* change your **attitude**, you will seek out **accountability**, and you will naturally start **acting** in ways that will guarantee more success as a writer than you have had to this point. Guaranteed.

Oh, one more thing. I need to address the excuses. We all use excuses and we really, really need to stop.

Chapter 8: Excuses to Eliminate

It's human nature to make excuses. Excuses are a way of soothing the pain of the cognitive dissonance that occurs when we're not doing what we're supposed to be doing. Excuses are a sort of defense mechanism. Think about it: rather than having to admit to yourself that you are doing something that is not right, or good for you, or that you are not doing something that you said you would do, you try to ease the pain by explaining and justifying your behavior or lack thereof. In this way, you believe you are protecting yourself from the pain of the truth.

But your brain is not truly fooled. You're just temporarily shifting the blame. In the long run, the excuses make you feel worse, because now you have added the pain of lying to yourself and others.

Excuses feed the pain of writer's block

Each year, literally millions of books go unpublished. You can blame this all you want on the gatekeepers, on the agents and publishers, and on the fact that publishers aren't willing to take a chance on new writers. In fact, writers are creative, and really good at coming up with great excuses. But the truth is, the biggest reason that these books go unpublished is that they were never finished. And why weren't they finished? Simple. The author quit.

Which excuses do authors who quit use, and how do you prevent this from happening to you?

EXCUSE: Lack of Time

First of all, here's the hard truth: in reality, we actually potentially have more time available to us than ever before, thanks to technology and other conveniences. We don't need to grow our own food, ride a buggy into town, or wash our clothes by hand. We don't even *really* need to talk on the phone. We've simply been drinking the Kool-Aid that tells us that "busy is good" and we're running on a treadmill of our own devising.

Make your writing time legitimate, not optional. It is as much a "real task" as your "day job" or housework.

Free time doesn't just happen. It isn't actually "free." You usually need to beg for, borrow, barter for, or steal that "free" time. And once you have done that, put it in your calendar.

Make writing a ritual, kind of like some people do for a bath. (You don't have time for a bath right now.) Make tea, light a candle, go to the same dedicated space. Over time, these signals will get your brain prepped for creative time faster. Psych yourself to do something similar when you get to the "business" stage of your book.

Compartmentalize. Literally. Shut the door, and then promise to yourself to shove any other concerns onto the figurative back burner while you write or take care of the business of being an author. This will definitely be easier to do if you schedule in a specific and manageable amount of time for this.

Combine writing with social time. Join a writing group that meets regularly for writing followed by conversation or create our own with old or new friends. This way you won't feel so solitary and you've just combined two time-consuming activities into one.

Give yourself a deadline. Kick start your writing with an external motivation like NaNoWriMo or a writing contest, which have to be completed by a certain date. Put this date in your calendar. Announce it on Instagram. Count down.

Consistency is key. The more regular you can make your writing, the more you can make it into a habit, the higher your chances of success. But "regularity" can mean daily, weekly, or three times a week. Whatever works for you. Just be realistic about how your choice of writing schedule will impact your progress.

Find your "magic hour." Most of us have a time of day when we are better at creative tasks, or more focused for editing or administrative work. Find what those hours are for you, for your writing and for the business side of writing: Is it early morning? Is it late at night? Is it your lunch hour? Don't let anyone try to tell you what is right for you, unless you feel truly incapable of figuring it out for yourself.

Here is my daily schedule:

Weekday:

6:30-7:30: Research and social media posts in bed. Knowing that the dog expects to be taken out by a certain hour provides a built-in time limit.
7:30-8:30: Dog out, more painful/boring business and marketing stuff to get it out of the way, while the espresso shots do their job.

8:30-9:30: Shower, checking on how the social media posts, responding to any messages and emails.

9:30-12:30: Writing, walk, lunch.

12:30-1:00: Email/social media follow up. Design side hustle tasks.

1:00-5:00: Writing/filming.

5:00-6:00: Walk dog, social media wrap up.

After dinner: Research and reading or relaxing.

Weekends:

Editing podcast & batching social media posts. Design side hustle. Eating too much and drinking too much wine.

If writing is your side hustle, your schedule will look very different, but that is totally fine.

Quit "obligations" that you wouldn't miss too much: that board or committee that drives you nuts, the book club that's more like an abuse session, the chore of cooking yet another meal when leftovers or takeout would do, the lion's share of the housework if you live in a home with other able-bodied people, the so-called social obligations that don't make you happy …beyond just taking up time, these things sap your energy and make you resentful. They can also bring about a slew of excuses of their own when you inevitably try to skip out on them. Better to "break up" cleanly.

What if you *still* can't find the time?

Time is not your real problem. Let's assume that we are not dealing with motivation block anymore, either. Your problem may be productivity. Productivity is basically how much you manage to do during the time you have. Being productive is one of the major keys to success, whether you are a writer or an entrepreneur or both or anything in between. Paying attention to common productivity mistakes is the first step to being more productive and successful.

How to be high performing? Let the perceived pain of the alternative show you the way.

Focus on minutes, not hours

An hour can get away from you. The pain of knowing you wasted time is way worse than the relatively small pain of making a highly detailed schedule for yourself. When you plan down to the minute, you can do more than you thought possible, and it's easier to change course if you see yourself being less productive than you could be.

Each day, list your top 3 tasks.

-One writing related.

-One marketing related.

-One home or self-care or organizational task.

If you have a main hustle or side hustle, sorry, but these 3 tasks are in addition to the other stuff you have to do. Remember when I said to focus on minutes?

In a single hour you can:

-Do a 25-minute Pomodoro technique-style writing sprint.

-Post content on your website and social media.

-Put a load of laundry in the washer.

Reverse engineer your success. And focus on the things that will get you there

Drop or postpone everything else. Do the 80-20 rule. Known as the Pareto Principle, it reminds us that in most cases, 80% of outcomes come from only 20% of activities. Ultra-productive people know which activities drive the greatest results. They focus on those and ignore the rest.

Will being president of the PTA help you to get to your dream of being an author? No? ditch it. Will playing Candy Crush do anything for your spot on the bestseller list? Absolutely not, right? You know what to do. Is going to an umpteenth hangout with your slacker friends going to help you to write? The pain of FOMO is less than the pain of failure. However, don't punish yourself and miss something truly special, like your best friend's engagement party or family Christmas because "I should be writing." That is not a balanced life.

Maintain balance

Could you get more done today? Probably. But if you forgo too much time with your family to tweak that paragraph that could definitely be addressed tomorrow, you are setting yourself up for a world of pain in the future. Yes, you may want to abbreviate your workouts when you are on a writing deadline. But completely obliterate balance and you are setting yourself up for a pain worse than writer's block.

Free your mind

Having a ton of stuff to keep track of in your head is a real pain. That's why you write it all down. In a calendar, in a notebook. It's a bit of a pain but only a momentary one compared to having it all bouncing around and poking at your brain.

Say "no"

You're a creative. You love new experiences and you love to make new connections, try new things. And/or maybe you're conscientious. If someone asks you for help: for editing, for a review, for a coffee date to pick your brain, you have a hard time turning them down. There is a pain that comes from missing out on something fun or a potential learning opportunity, or from being afraid of being perceived as selfish or unhelpful.

Again, how will the majority of these opportunities or obligations help your writing career in the long run? Most of them will not. Karma will not bite you in the ass if you don't review yet another book this month. At this stage in the game, you've paid your dues. It's your turn. Imagine the pain of knowing that, if you'd only succeeded more, you could have made more of an impact by sending the elevator back down. With practice, you'll ease the pain and guilt of saying no and savor the pleasure of saying yes when it actually means more to you.

Try "theme days"

Each day of the week you can focus on major areas- both in your writing itself and in your promotions, and in your life as a writer. Yes, you have your "schedule," like the one I elaborated on earlier, but there can be a theme driving the content within that schedule. Here's pretty much how my week works:

-Monday: Catch up/set up day

On this day, I do everything I can to set myself up for the week. I address any loose ends from the weekend, create and batch content to be released on social media throughout the rest of the week if I didn't get to it on the weekend, determine specific writing tasks, and write my to-do list, including planning a few challenges such as signing up for writing events or reaching out to media outlets. I'll also check on my outline and make sure it still has everything it needs and fill in some blanks in my work in progress. Monday night: I film my podcast.

-Tuesday: Social Media Push

On Tuesdays, a Creative Happy Hour podcast episode gets released to YouTube and to all the podcasting platforms such as Spotify, iHeartRadio, and Apple Podcasts. I'll double check that it posted properly and get to work in the morning promoting it on all platforms including Facebook pages and groups, Instagram, Pinterest, and LinkedIn. I'll tie the creative theme in with books and writing, and post that on my Spalmorum platform. I'll have pre-planned much of this content, so it doesn't take long. With that stressful part behind me, I'll do Pomodoro style writing sprints and answer any comments on social media as a break. Once I'm wiped from writing, in the late afternoon or evening, I will flesh out the topic for my writing group, which often incorporates some of the research for the podcast.

-Wednesday: Writing Coaching Day

In the morning I create a full outline for my writing group lesson. I hold writing group from noon to 2. When I get home, I use the outline to do a video recap so I can share the day's lesson with more people via YouTube. I brainstorm on how to take my own advice and integrate the lessons from writing group into my work. I tweak any applicable sections of my work in progress. I update my "writing to-do list."

-Thursday: Sprint Day

This is a long, busy day. I edit & post the video recap I shot the day before and create the graphics for it and do a social media push for both that video and the podcast. I make myself do this pretty fast, so I don't waste any time on it. After this, I'm usually feeling inspired and exhausted at the same time, so I do writing sprints to try to get ahead without agonizing over my work too much.

-Friday: Wrapping up the week

I take Friday morning to edit the podcast video, to upload audio and video versions of it and schedule it for release on various platforms including YouTube, Apple Podcasts, Spotify, and iHeartRadio. I also create the thumbnails and any other graphics I need. Friday before the end of day, I make sure to address any emails or administrative tasks that popped up. I write down anything that needs to be done the next week. Usually by this point I have less energy, so I focus on rewrites, so I can feel like I am in a good place on Monday.

-Saturday & Sunday: Recharge & reset

On these days, I do the majority of my reading and research, and I enjoy creative field trips and family and friend time. Ideally, I'll also do some leisurely free writing. This is a good time for brainstorming new ideas, because I'm feeling more relaxed and creative.

*Pay attention to your levels. (Energy, Mood)

You can't make more minutes in the day but protecting your energy and mood will increase your attention, focus, creativity, prioritizing skills, and overall productivity. Successful authors don't skip meals, sleep, or breaks. This is why you pick the correct time of day to do certain tasks, this is why you need to recharge, and this is why a good balance of writing sprints and leisurely writing can be a good idea.

What if you've set aside the time, but you get stuck?

This is the situation that pretty much illustrates the conventional definition of writer's block: you're sitting there, you've set aside the time to write, but the words aren't flowing.

With our new, more inclusive definition of writer's block, I hope that you realize that if one piece of the success puzzle isn't happening today, you can always complete another piece:

Write a blog post or answer a question on Quora

The informal aspect will take the pressure off, but this is still helping to build your platform.

Go online

Yeah, we know we told you to unplug, but now that you're stuck, you might as well post on Facebook or Instagram and/or interact with other writers on a board or on Twitter. That doesn't mean you should do an hour deep dive into the black hole of posts.

Organize

Your desk. Your in-box. Your desktop. Your document folders. Your upcoming vacation. Maybe you'll gain clarity.

Meditate

Or stretch. Or have a snack. Whatever calms and centers you.

Read

A book, not a gossip mag or articles that overanalyze your writer's block and make you feel bad about yourself. Your reading can be research or just for fun. No matter what, it'll inspire you and feed your creativity. You can also listen to a podcast but avoid anything "noisy" that is just a distraction. And no, no TV.

EXCUSE: Perfectionism

Authors who blame perfectionism claim that they're afraid their work is never good enough. Of course it isn't good enough. Our work is *never* as good as we'd hoped. It never lives up to the ideal we have in our heads and hearts. And that is why we keep trying. That is called being a passionate realist.

The perfectionist is far from perfect. They think they have found a virtuous excuse: They won't finish their book out of an excess of respect for their poor readers, whom they want to spare from something sub-divine. This is silly. I know so many people who claim perfectionism, but then when you look at all other aspects of their lives, they demonstrate laziness and procrastination even in areas where perfection is not expected nor required. They claim they spend too much time self-doubting and revising everything to death before they are even done. But in truth, so many of them have not even gotten to that stage. If you "know" this self-editing urge will happen to you, outsmart yourself by racing ahead and getting absolutely everything you can on paper before you are tempted to over-edit it all. Also, save an intact version of your work in case you take too much out. But otherwise, see perfectionism for what it is: an excuse.

EXCUSE: It's happening too slowly

One minute, you're raring to go, and the next, you are discouraged because this is taking much, much longer than you thought. You're going to try to use it as an excuse to quit, aren't you? Don't do that. This is just a very transparent excuse!

Or maybe you finish your draft, but your impatience hurts you because you're not willing to spend time on edits. Honestly, you're just going to have to cultivate some patience. Or trick yourself by working on several manuscripts at a time. Or give yourself less time to write. Go about your normal busy day, only busier, and only allow yourself half an hour to write. Eventually you may get frustrated that you only have half an hour a day to write your awesome story, and you hopefully will get motivated again.

EXCUSE: Loneliness

Sound familiar?

"I'm super lonely, and I've been ignoring my friends, so I need to hang out with them more rather than write…"

Why did you spend all your time partying and hanging out with your friends instead of writing your book? Because you were lonely. Painfully lonely. Poor you. Human contact is a need, not a want, right? Writing is so solitary. You don't often get positive affirmations unless you go looking for them. It can be hard to continue without support. Well, go and find some support. There are writing groups in every town, online or off. And if your town is one of the ones that literally doesn't have a writing group, it sounds like it's such a boring place to live that people will jump at the chance to attend if you start one.

If you ask a bunch of writers what the worst thing about writing is, the majority will tell you the worst thing is the loneliness. The solitude. Everyone needs friends! Sure, you need to concentrate and focus, and alone time is an integral part of the writing life, but without the balance of human interaction and physical activity interspersed with intense creative production, you might feel like you're working in a void.

So get some writer friends. They can keep you on schedule. After all, the definition of a writer is someone who writes. So, if you're getting distracted and not doing that, and no one is there to call you out on it, you can get away from your purpose without even realizing it. The other good part of having a writing community is meeting up and writing somewhere- knowing there will be company will motivate you to show up, and all those people typing away will ensure that you actually produce some work- if you're sitting just staring at your screen, someone might call you out!

Your writer friends will probably love to read, too, so there's a good chance that if you have a relationship with them, they'll want to read your book. They can also be your critique group, your preliminary editors, and your cheerleaders, both on social media and in real life.

But truly, you can still see your non-writing friends. If you treat writing like a job, you should still be able to pencil in time for happy hour.

EXCUSE: Writing is really, really hard.

If it was easy everyone would be doing it, because finishing a book is an amazing feeling. But writing being too "hard" doesn't really fly, because some people do it every day. Some people are super successful at it, and I'm pretty sure that never once did a super successful author say, "Oh, writing? Yeah, it's super easy!"

If you find yourself trotting out the old "writing is too hard" excuse one too many times, you might actually want to consider quitting. Most writers know writing is hard, but they still need to do it. If that's not the case, writing might not be for you right now. Why don't you give it a break for a while and circle back if your story is still calling to you.

Or maybe you should stick it out. I would venture to say that writing is even harder for the better writers, because they respect the process and the depths they must plumb to write something that touches their readers. So if writing is super hard, congrats. You're meant to do this.

EXCUSE: You've fallen out of love with the story.

Wait. You were excited enough about this story to start writing it in the first place. Are you saying that your idea fooled you into thinking it was good? You've fallen out of love, but this is definitely a "it's not you, it's me" scenario. Your poor story didn't do anything wrong. This is all on you. Seems that you just don't know how to express your story. Seems like you didn't follow advice and base your story on a compelling character. Wait! Wait- you didn't write an outline, did you? Oh boy.

People fall out of love with a story for the same reasons they fall out of love with a person:

Distance

Does absence make the heart grow fonder? Not really. It usually leads to infidelity. You've been away from your work for too long, and now you're thinking of cheating on it with something else. Try to remember why you fell in love with it. Maybe you should spend more time with your book. The good news is, you don't have to buy a plane ticket to see your manuscript.

Seeing flaws

After the first flames of passion cool down, you start to be less forgiving of flaws. You start to get triggered by every little imperfection. Maybe this is a signal that you should fix some of the problems with your story. So much easier than trying to fix a romantic partner.

Boredom

Same old, same old. Eventually you get bored. Time to shake it up a little, to make things more exciting. Give your characters a makeover, give them a new setting to operate in. The beauty of being a writer is that this is all free, and it's all in your power.

An old flame resurfaces

You're happy with your story, you are. But then something makes you think of that old project you never saw through to the end. Did you give up on it too early? Could there be anything there? Is it actually better than the story you have now? If you give in to the urge to see what will happen when you rekindle that old love affair, just know that the issues that made you break up with it the first time never magically go away, and know that your current project will suffer majorly from this turn of events.

EXCUSE: I can't do it now because I'm waiting for the right time.

EXCUSE: I'm too tired/stressed.

EXCUSE: I'm not good at self-promotion.

EXCUSE: The chances for success are so slim that I'd better not even start.

Sorry, but if you've gotten this far, you know that these are not valid. They are just excuses. If you're pissed off at me for not offering in-depth explanations for each one, go back and read the beginning of the section. You didn't pay attention. OK, OK fine. For those of you who are really concerned about the whole "odds of success" thing, the next chapter is for you.

The 3 questions that kill every excuse, every time:

The next time you try to use an excuse to get out of moving forward with your writing, write it down, read it several times out loud, and ask yourself:

1) Would I think this excuse was a good one if I heard anyone else saying it?

2) Does this excuse actually make sense in any way?

3) Is this it? Am I really going to let this silly excuse stop me?

Chapter 9: A "system" to ensure your book's success

First of all, let me just say that I get it: we are more likely to do something when we know that our odds of success are higher- we work harder if we know there is a bonus on the line, we work out more if we are promised results, we buy the grass seed in the bag that claims it will grow in both Siberia and the Sahara. It's human nature... We are always looking for an easy way out, a formula, a set of directions that will make our progression from just starting to success easier and more foolproof.

Yet... yet we still play the lottery, we still fall in love and get married, we still gamble in Vegas...and most of the time, we don't insist on a secret foolproof formula for that stuff- so why not put in the work and see where your book goes? It's better odds than the lottery.

But I get it:

-We writers want to eliminate the risk of working really hard on something and falling flat on our faces.

-We want to lessen the chance for failure, and the anticipated pain that will stem from it.

-We don't want to embarrass ourselves by putting all of our hopes and dreams into something, only to have it fall flat.

-We want to give ourselves the best possible chances for success.

-Making a task easier makes it more likely we will get it done.

-Taking out the guesswork saves us time.

Therefore, formulas, methods, and systems are everywhere: For losing weight, for building an email list, for learning a language. And yes, a great many writers ask about the formula for writing a best-selling novel. If there truly were such a formula, all novels would be best sellers. However, just like the examples of people asking for advice and not taking it, just because somebody knows how to do something, doesn't mean that they will do it that way.

So, with no further ado, I am going to deliver some factors which will vastly increase the level of success, at least the commercial success, of your novel. It is up to you to decide to implement this knowledge.

Readability

What do I mean by that? I literally mean that you want to eliminate any thing that stands in the way of your readers absorbing your story.

-How is your grammar?

-How easy is it to understand your writing?

-How directly does your writing help the reader to understand your story, and the world you are trying to describe?

Many writers think that they need to have sophisticated and complex sentences, and that their vocabulary needs to be intellectual, that their words need to be unique. That is simply not true. Most best sellers are written at a 6th to 10th grade level. Of course, if you want to make your writing more poetic than that, that is your prerogative. However, it does not increase the readability of your book, and it is readability that will make you a mainstream success. A good editor can help you with readability, by eliminating any confusing phrasing, making sure to fill in details that may be missing for comprehension, and by making sure that your grammar and formatting are correct. Also, an editor will make sure that details are correct, that names and places remain consistent, and that dialogue is clear.

Complex characters

The reason many readers fall in love with a specific book, or a series, is that they identify with one or several of the characters. Why do people identify with the character? It has to do with their complexity. Nobody loves a character that is too simple. What does that mean? It means that your character is too good, too gifted, too smart, too pretty. No one wants to read about that. Your character should have weaknesses, they should have doubts, and they should definitely experience a change or progression as your storyline progresses. Spend a lot of time on your characters, because they will drive everything in your book. Even your villain should be complex and subtle. Every section of dialogue should show how characters interact with each other, how they battle each other or doubt each other, or how they need each other.

Dialogue

Dialogue can make or break your book. Dialogue is actually incredibly difficult to get right. The best way to write good dialogue? Listen in on other people's conversations. Notice the pacing, notice the words that get left out. Notice how people don't constantly refer back to things that should be understood, how they don't use each other's names repeatedly.

The difference between a dialogue in your book and a dialogue in real life is that the conversations in your book need to have a specific purpose. They need to reflect a conflict, a goal, or something that otherwise moves the plot forward. Otherwise, they are simply not needed.

Also, if you're wondering which words make good synonyms for *said*, the answer is none of them! "Said" is unobtrusive, and people do not notice it, as opposed to a synonym, which will make people pause in their reading. This goes back to our readability concept. You don't want to give people obstacles that make them pause in their enjoyment of your book. You can make an occasional exception, of course...if it's important for your character to yell something, or whisper it, have them do that. Just don't obsess over finding odd words to express it. They don't need to holler, bellow, vociferate, bawl, or squeak.

Dialogue is one of those things that you are really going to practice for the entirety of your writing career. You will want to read it out loud to yourself, you will want to question it, have others read it, and give it in enormous amount of thought.

Plot

You might have thought that plot would be number one on my list, but funnily enough, it's not. You can make almost any plot work well if you have fantastic characters.

That being said, let's take a look at plot. If you come up with a great plot, a great story that will inspire readers, that is definitely one of the elements that will help your book to be successful. How can you tell whether your plot is a good one?

Create an elevator pitch for it and test it on numerous people around you. Does it awaken their curiosity and pique their interest? Does it sound too similar to something that has already been done? You may need to tweak that plot, you don't necessarily need to throw the whole thing out, but you need something that will differentiate it. Play around with your plot and story line until you land on one that is truly inspiring and that can be carried through a whole book. Make sure the plot elements will cause of the characters to grow and change, that it will challenge them enough to keep it interesting.

Pacing

Pacing is a key element as well. Read a book that has been made into a movie. Then go see the movie. Check out the choices that the director made, and how they chose to tell the story from the book in film form. Movies are usually great examples of how pacing works. Are you kept on the edge of your seat? Are there moments that are a little boring? Usually, those are taken out of the movie, just as they should be taken out of a book if you wish for it to be a bestseller. Moments of quiet reflection are interesting, and can be very artful, and can be wonderful to read about, but if what you are looking for is commercial success, you may want to cut them short.

It seems a little harsh, but many readers just want to be entertained. They essentially want a movie in written form.

"But wait," you might be thinking. "I don't want to write that kind of book."

You don't have to write that kind of book. But then keep in mind that you are making a decision that will potentially impact your book's commercial success.

Of course, you could argue that some books that end up being huge commercial successes have a slow, thoughtful tone. This is true, of course, but if you really look at their pacing, it is expertly done. Something about those books keeps the reader reading.

If you are an experienced writer, you may already have figured out how to do this, however, if you are a little bit new to this, it is much easier to keep up pacing with action. You also will want to make sure to provide balance between action, dialogue, and description. Your book should not have any moments that stagnate. Each scene should have a goal. That is pacing. Even your language and sentence structure will contribute to the pacing.

A unique world

Oftentimes, readers are drawn in by a world that fascinates them. Think of the Lord of the Rings, or Harry Potter, or The Twilight series, or Downton Abbey... They each explore a world that is described in detail, that has both differences and similarities to ours, and which shapes the behavior and choices of the characters.

You can completely invent a world, or you can borrow one from something that you know well or have observed, but make sure to flesh out the details so that your reader is drawn in. Make sure that the environment and the world are richly layered.

Careful: you don't need to describe it all at once. In general, only the elements that are crucial to your story should make their way into a specific scene. Show how your characters interact with their environment.

Purpose

Purpose is one of the most important factors when it comes to your chances of writing success. I know that this whole section was about a formula that makes it more likely for your book to be commercially successful, but focusing on the wrong purpose, for example, writing your book so you can become famous and make lots of money, can set you up for failure. Be honest with yourself on what your true writer's purpose is. You may want to re-visit the chapter on motivation for more on this.

There is nothing wrong with wanting to make money from your writing, or to be known for your writing, but that will be a by-product of your writing and publishing a good book.

Conclusion

You went through the Spalmorum Method. You were super honest about your mindsets, your foibles, and your excuses. You figured out which specific pains were resulting from the specific blocks your mindsets were causing. You learned to reframe the mindsets, ditch your excuses, and seek out accountability. You started to take the actions that move you towards success. Yet you have a niggling fear that those blocks are not completely gone, or that they will resurface. What to do then?

"I got blocked again. Is this it? Am I not meant to do this writing thing after all?

This thought itself is causing you pain. The fear of suddenly having lost your creativity, having lost the thing that defined you, the thing that gave you purpose… Losing that purpose is painful. The fear compounds the pain. At this point, you're probably internally panicking. We need to deal with the problem, stat! Let's cover all of the bases so that we can get permanently get you out of this difficult situation.

But wait, you say.

It actually doesn't hurt anymore.

You don't feel the pain anymore? You're actually OK with it?

Hell no, you're not OK with it. You've actually simply found some kind of coping mechanism to make you numb. Numbness is not the goal. Ever. Even at the dentist's office, numbness is temporary, and usually still pretty uncomfortable. Where did you pain go? There is no way it just went away. Even if we end up concluding that you are truly not meant to be a writer (doubtful, if you've made it this far in the book), there is still pain associated with having lost your purpose. If you're feeling numb, let's literally find that pain again. let's use that pain to get you fired up for something, whether that thing is writing or not.

Are you ready for some more radical honesty?

Let's examine why you feel like your creativity has gone away.

First of all, **is it the passion that's lacking, or is it the work ethic?**

Does your sudden loss of inspiration and motivation simply coincide with the discovery that this whole writing, publishing, and marketing process takes a really long time and a lot of hard work? Have you finally realized that success in writing is not a function of luck and fairy dust, but rather a long slog in the trenches? I get it: when you're working your hardest, and you feel like your chances of success are tenuous, it's easy to convince yourself that you're maybe wasting your time.

Go back and re-examine the reality of the situation:

-If you quit at the beginning of the process, or halfway through, or when you're nearly there, you haven't succeeded in the strictest sense. You can't call yourself an author. Sorry, but it's true. However, your time and energy were not truly wasted. You still have something to show for them. And you can always pick those elements, those seeds of a book, up again and finally make them bloom into something great.

-If you finished your book and it did not succeed, you didn't actually do everything you could do. You have succeeded in the simple act of writing a book. You can call yourself an author. And any extra work you do will doubtless move you closer to success. No time wasted in that.

-If you finished your book and it did all right, but it did not get the accolades you had hoped it would, you have three choices: keep improving that book, write another book, or quit. How does the thought of each of those options make you feel?

This is also a good time to re-examine whether you have enough of a support system. Remember when you read that you should join a writing group, and you still didn't join the writing group? Join the writing group. You will finally see that you're not alone, you'll start to notice the differences between the writers who keep talking about the book they want to write, and the writers who actually put in the work to write that book. They are two very different animals. Which one do you want to be? It's fine to be either one, but if you have even a tiny bit of the pain associated with not writing your book, you should try to be the author that actually goes ahead and writes the book.

Many of you are wondering if your inspiration will ever come back.

Is this a permanent situation? Are you going to feel dumb for the rest of your life? I really doubt that. Most creative people are fed by creativity. They're fed by the excitement of working on something and of being fired up about a story or a painting or a building or a piece of music. Once you remove whatever is causing the block, once you address the mindset that is causing this problem, your inspiration will probably return. There's a chance that it is going to return and push you to work on a different type of creative work. But really be honest with yourself as to whether that is OK with you. Are you just trying to rationalize quitting?

Remember, you are allowed to take a break.

There is no honor in having a complete breakdown. Let go of the guilt, but don't bury the guilt. Also, are you expecting writing to be everything for you? Are you expecting it to fill the void of everything else?

Has something changed in your life?

A lot can change in a writer's life. We wouldn't be human if those things didn't affect us. Did you change jobs? Lose your job? Lose a friend? Did your child move out? Did you go through a breakup? Has something changed in your health? Do you think that yes, you might be depressed? All of these things can absolutely impact your writing and your motivation.

Be kind to yourself. Sometimes circumstances demand our full attention. Let go of the guilt.

Do the motivation questionnaire again. If something has changed in your motivation, it will be helpful to understand it more fully.

Look for patterns in your thinking or behavior, or trends in your life.

True Story Part 2

Here's a small snapshot of what has happened in my life in the past ten years:

2010-2011

We are living outside of San Francisco, after a move from London. I'm **working as a magazine writer and editor and doing freelance writing projects.** I've had my PhD for 8 years but haven't really done anything with it. Two books I'd written years earlier have been sitting idle in my computer's hard drive after a few rejections and despite requests from agents to see more. Someone introduces me to an agent who really likes one of the books. **I have the book edited. I sign with the agent.** Life is great.

2012-2013

We decide to renovate our family home. I act as general contractor. Our four-person family and our two dogs move into my one-bedroom art studio for four months during the work. The literary agent decides to cut me loose. **I self-publish 2 books** but don't promote them. My husband gets injured and leaves his job. We sell our home, take our kids out of the school they love, move across the country, and put them in a new school. We renovate an old house (I act as designer and contractor) while we live in a haunted cottage with no internet. I open a retail shop from scratch.

2014-2015

Just when we finally finish renovating and moving into the house, my husband accepts a job across the country. He moves to LA while I stay behind to organize things in Virginia. We rent a townhouse in LA, get our son into school in LA, get our daughter into boarding school on the East Coast, and when school is over, we spend the summer in LA. I fly back to settle daughter into school in Virginia and deal with shop details, hire a manager, and then fly back to settle my son into his new LA school. I embark on a Palm Springs house flipping project, which has me driving to Palm Springs twice a week while my son is in school to act as designer and general contractor while running the shop at a distance. I take my books off of Amazon because I decide I want to publish conventionally, after all. But I don't do anything else about it because I am so busy with my shop and design clients and projects.

2015-2016

I sell the house in Palm Springs after an extended legal battle. We buy a house in LA. We get our son into a boarding school on the East coast. We become empty nesters. I freak out. **I rework and have one of my books edited again. I get a publishing deal.** I lose the publishing deal. I close my shop. **I work on some scripts.** Life is good for about 6 months. Then my husband loses his job.

2017-2018

We sell the LA house, do another cross-country move. I give up on my scripts. I reopen a new shop and creative space. I take on more design clients. **I start Spalmorum. I start coaching writers. I start reworking my old books again and start on two new ones.** I still have no internet. My daughter applies to college and decides to go to school in California. Our dog dies.

Late 2018-2020

I make the decision to move so I can take my career more seriously. (I can't live on the East Coast in the middle of nowhere with no Internet, but this might have been something of an excuse, I know.) **I launch my author tube channel on YouTube. I do NaNoWriMo.** I close my shop/creative space. We move back to the SF area into a tiny rented house. **I put a moratorium on construction so I can focus on writing.** I help my son with college applications. **I start my writing group. I start my podcast. I write this book**, while **working on 3 other novels,** I do **editing work for other writers. I keep growing my author platform. I decide to publish books through my own publishing company, Spalmorum.**

Sound chaotic? I'm not even including other good and bad stuff: extensive travel (think at least one cross-country or international trip a month), family drama, deaths of friends and family, legal issues, and a couple of tax audits.

Maybe your life in the past ten years has been more settled, maybe crazier. This isn't a contest. What I'm trying to say is that we all go through shit.

But look at the general trend in my recap of the past ten years. **Positive writing-related stuff is bolded for clarity.** At first, my forays into writing and publishing are tentative. I get an agent. I lose an agent. I self-publish, I take it down, I get a publishing deal, I lose it, I write some scripts, they get some traction, but I stop pushing when I leave LA.

But then, something changes. My mindset changes. And I start focusing and doing everything to move my writing career forward. That momentum builds on itself. Look at the entry for the most recent years. Almost everything is bolded. The vast majority of my efforts are put towards writing-related activities.

The luck that you generate when you start to focus your energy on your writing builds on itself. The traction your platform gains builds on itself. You move forward, plain and simple.

I'm not one of those people who is going to tell you "I am a mega bestselling author of a bazillion books and I've figured out the exact secret so you can follow my formula and be exactly like me!"

No, I'm telling you that I am like most of you- with a chaotic life, and doubts, and responsibilities, and shit hitting the fan, and setbacks. And I've changed my mindset and started moving forward. No excuses. No way around it. There are moments when my progress gets slowed by this thing called life, but you know, life happens. Yet writing is part of our lives.

So, if life is tough, if it's all of a sudden super crazy and hard, and your inspiration or motivation have dried up, don't add to the pain of being unproductive by freaking out that your muse and your will to write will never come back. Just keep your eye on the prize.

When I'm going nuts because of the constant sheer unpredictability of life, it's nice to know that if I sit down and write a paragraph or post on my author platform, I've done something to move myself in a positive direction as a writer.

And guys, life is hard, and there are other pain points that you will hit. If nothing ever seems to be working in the writing department, and you've sincerely given it your all, maybe writing is not meant to be your thing right now. Maybe there is something else that will fire you up and make you want to succeed in all kinds of ways. Test that thought: Does the excitement of embarking on something new fire you up and ease the pain of not writing? Well then go forth, baby. The great news is that all of the mindset hacks and other tips you found in this book will help you with that, too.

For those of you who can't quit won't quit, thanks so much for reading this book. I can't wait to see what you do with your new unblocked hearts and minds. Please keep in touch with me at www.spalmorum.com. You can sign up for weekly pep talks and videos into your mailbox. And if you're ready to truly put your newfound mindset into action, and want just a little more, you can always reach out…I'll be there!

Your life as a successful author starts today.

Xoxo,

Karena